MEXICO

Coatepec
Mexico City Jalapa
Cholula Veracruz
Puebla Tlacotalpan

GUATEMALA
Guatemala City

EL SALVADOR
San José
COSTA RICA

HONDURAS
Tegucigalpa

NICARAGUA
Bluefields
Managua

PANAMA
Panama City

JAMAICA
Kingston

HAITI
Port-au-Prince

DOMINICAN
REPUBLIC
Santo
Domingo

PUERTO RICO
San Juan

ATLANTIC

OCEAN

Santa Marta
Barranquilla
Cartagena

Maracaibo
CURAÇAO
Puerto Cabello
Caracas
Valencia Cumaná
Barquisimeto

Port of Spain
TRINIDAD & TOBAGO

BR. GUIANA
Georgetown
SURINAM
Paramaribo
FR. GUIANA
Cayenne

Bucaramanga Mérida
Medellín
Tunja
Bogotá
COLOMBIA
Cali
Popayán

VENEZUELA

ECUADOR
Quito
Guayaquil Ambato

PERU

Lima

Cuzco

Arequipa

BOLIVIA
La Paz
Cochabamba
Oruro Santa Cruz
Sucre
Potosí

Tarija

PARAGUAY
Asunción

BRAZIL

Brasília

Belém

Fortaleza

Recife

Salvador

Belo Horizonte

São Paulo
Curitiba

Vitória

Rio de Janeiro

Pôrto Alegre

Córdoba

URUGUAY

Santiago

Concepción

Temuco

Buenos Aires
Montevideo

CHILE

ARGENTINA

PACIFIC

OCEAN

ATLANTIC

OCEAN

STECHERT-HAFNER OFFICES

LATIN AMERICA

PLACES COVERED BY LACAP,

1960-1967

EQUATORIAL SCALE

0   500   1000   1500
MILES

0   500   1000   1500
KILOMETRES

The Latin American Cooperative Acquisitions Program....

AN IMAGINATIVE VENTURE

by M. J. Savary

19 68

HAFNER PUBLISHING COMPANY, INC.

NEW YORK

First printing 1968

Printed and Published by
HAFNER PUBLISHING COMPANY, INC.
31 East 10th Street
New York, N.Y. 10003

Library of Congress Card Catalogue Number: 68-19791

COMPOSITION BY TOPEL TYPOGRAPHIC CORP., N.Y.C.

Printed in U.S.A. by
NOBLE OFFSET PRINTERS, INC.
NEW YORK 3, N. Y.

To all those who made this book possible

. . . The hopes and despairs
connected with original work
are alike fallacious, . . . one's
work is never so bad as it appears
on bad days, nor so good as it
appears on good days.

Bertrand Russell, *Autobiography*

Table of Contents

Foreword

The efforts of American librarians to develop collections on a grand scale to serve scholars and researchers have been described in various books and periodical literature of the profession. The bibliography and references included in this volume by Mrs. Savary will provide some idea of these approaches. The conferences that have been held on acquisitions work and collection building have become more specific in recent years, and have concentrated on the different parts of the world. The Farmington Plan, the PL 480 acquisition program, and the earlier Library of Congress Cooperative Acquisitions project come to mind. Robert Vosper and Robert Talmadge have written in detail of the Farmington Plan, and there is no doubt that the results of the PL 480 project will be described fully in the future.

It is gratifying to have the Latin American Cooperative Acquisitions Program studied completely by Mrs. Savary. The author, who started on this investigation as a master's essay, has been, as the reader will observe, enthusiastic about the preparation of this manuscript for the use of the library profession. Although the sponsorship of LACAP has been that of a commercial firm, Stechert-Hafner, Inc., the approach of the writer has been quite objective. The resolutions of commendation adopted at the several (now 12) Seminars on the Acquisition of Latin American Library Materials (SALALM) are associated with the name of Dominick Coppola, of Stechert-Hafner, and of others in the Company who sought to assist librarians in a most difficult area of the world in the matter of acquisitions. With the mention of Mr. Coppola's name, it appears necessary to call attention to two other persons who helped at the beginning to activate the LACAP program, Robert E. Kingery, and Marietta Daniels Shepard whose efforts in the Latin American field led to the development of the program. One could list many other individuals who participated, and Mrs. Savary has done this well.

This volume should be helpful to librarians of research libraries not only for the specific information concerning Latin American publications and their acquisitions in United States libraries, but also for the consideration given to the place of Latin America in the world book trade, the special characteristics of the book trade in Latin American countries, the movement to develop bibliographical guides to the literature, and the over-all efforts to develop cooperative acquisitions programs. The distinctive contribution of the book, however, is the assessment, after an historical framework has been set, of LACAP.

Undoubtedly, the project would not have been successful if there had not been men and women who were available to press constantly, sometimes against what seemed to be ultimate frustration. The work of Nettie Lee Benson, Guillermo Baraya Borda, Dominick Coppola, A. W. Bork, and others is reported on in minute detail. It is an astonishing story of relentless book hunting, and one can only admire the accomplishments of the group of people who were involved. The successful "Traveling Agent" is pin-pointed with remarkable clarity, and resourcefulness and stamina are among the important ingredients of this individual.

Mrs. Savary has given us an informative work, based on a careful review of relevant documents and reports, as well as on the correspondence she examined and personal interviews she held. The results should enable those active in the program to improve it, and also they should serve as a blueprint for effective activity for the future.

Maurice F. Tauber

Preface

There are three ways of attacking a vast subject. One can go from the general to the particular; one can start with the particular and broaden out; or one can plunge in in midstream. The third solution has been adopted here.

The subject of LACAP first cropped up when the writer was doing some reading on the international exchange of publications. As the developments leading to the adoption of the UNESCO conventions in 1958 were described, there were frequent references to the subject of cooperative acquisitions, and to the Seminars on the Acquisition of Latin American Library Materials (SALALM). There were also some references to LACAP, but it was usually dismissed with some such comment as "This, being a commercial program, does not concern us here."

Curious, the author decided to find out more. LACAP turned out to be the Latin American Cooperative Acquisitions Project (now Program), run by Stechert-Hafner, Inc., international booksellers. It had originated in SALALM, and it was one manifestation of a trend towards cooperative acquisition which had been evident in the United States for over a century. Both the magnitude of the schemes themselves—the Farmington Plan, for instance—and the scale of the thinking behind them are impressive.

The author was seeking a subject that would fit tidily into the limitations of a master's paper in library science for the Graduate Library School of Long Island University, and for that reason—apart from its intrinsic interest—LACAP was chosen. Some of the background of cooperative acquisitions was sketched in, but the focus of the study was LACAP itself. This book, which is based on the master's paper, is therefore strictly limited in scope. It does not attempt to give the history of cooperative acquisitions in the United States, fascinating as that would be to tell. It is not even an exhaustive study of LACAP. It concentrates on the origin and history of the Program and the procurement of current monographs by Latin American authors. The period covered is 1960 to mid-1967. Some reference is made to other library materials—

institutional publications, for instance—and to the activities of other groups and bodies—SALALM, the Library of Congress, the Farmington Plan—but only insofar as they impinge on LACAP. There is no intention to disregard these activities or to minimize their importance. It is a question of light and shade. Here, the spotlight is on LACAP.

As cooperative acquisition has seen its greatest flowering in the United States, and as LACAP is run by an American firm, this study deals with developments in the United States. Contributions to the literature of cooperative acquisitions from other countries —notably England—have been ignored except when they have borne directly on LACAP. Furthermore, as this is the history of an American program, it is directed mainly to librarians in the United States. "American" therefore means "North American." "Latin American" is used to refer to all the countries south of the Rio Grande, and "South American" to designate only those which belong to the South American continent. The account of difficulties and developments in the Latin American book trade involves neither criticism nor a value judgment of methods which often differ widely from those of the United States. Rather, the facts are given with a strong feeling of sympathy and indebtedness to the countries of Latin America, from whose vitality, warmth, and individuality the writer foresees many joys to come.

In order not to overburden the text and fatigue the reader, footnotes have for the most part been avoided and traceable references included in the text. There would be little point, in any event, in referring the reader to unpublished materials, such as letters, and reports in the files of Stechert-Hafner. The SALALM reports and papers that are mentioned can easily be found in the SALALM records, now regularly published by the Pan American Union. For those who are interested in tracking down references, the original paper, which was thoroughly documented, is available on microfilm from the Graduate Library School of Long Island University, C. W. Post College, Brookville, Long Island, New York.

Although every effort has been made to keep this study as objective and factual as possible, the author has found it impossible to avoid a certain bias. It is difficult not to be enthusiastic about an imaginative scheme which is a real breakthrough in Latin American acquisitions. Furthermore, the magnitude of the aim and the caliber of the people involved are impressive. The firm of

Stechert-Hafner took a financial risk in launching the Program and has made it a viable concern. Dr. Nettie Lee Benson, the well known Latin American historian and head of the Latin American collection of the University of Texas, spent many courageous and tiring months pioneering for LACAP and laying the firm foundation on which it subsequently operated. Guillermo Baraya Borda, who took up where she left off, has traveled all over Latin America and displayed both good humor and perspicacity in the face of many difficulties. Both he and Dr. Benson have described their experiences in some of the most interesting reports that it has ever been the author's good fortune to read. Walter H. Hafner, Chairman of the Board of Stechert-Hafner, Inc., and his brother, the late Otto H. Hafner, President of the Hafner Publishing Company—personalities in their own right—have been actively concerned with the scheme. Dominick Coppola, now President of Stechert-Hafner, Inc., an MS from Columbia University's School of Library Service, has been the mainspring of the Program from the beginning. He did some of the traveling and investigation reported here, and he has been responsible for the day-to-day decisions, the unobtrusive administrative work, and the streamlining of procedures which have transformed LACAP from an experimental project into a permanent program.

They have achieved something, and they merit a salute.

Apart from the people immediately concerned with LACAP, there are others to whom it is impossible to remain indifferent. The sound good sense, lucid intelligence, and outstanding organizing ability of Mrs. Marietta Daniels Shepard, Associate Librarian of the Columbus Memorial Library and Permanent Secretary of SALALM, can come as no surprise to those who know anything of SALALM's achievements. LACAP owes a great deal to her encouragement, interest, and advice, and the author to her unfailing helpfulness and patience. The record of her achievements, like that of Dr. Benson's, excites both admiration and gratitude.

As exciting as SALALM and LACAP—and therefore as difficult to view with icy objectivity—are the vast schemes launched by the Library of Congress and the Association of Research Libraries. The Library of Congress has initiated many programs of its own —the program under Public Law 480 and the National Program for Acquisitions and Cataloging, for instance—and it has been, and is, a participant in many others, including the Farmington

Plan, run by the Association of Research Libraries, and LACAP. In relation to Latin America, the role of the Hispanic Foundation is self-evident. Its activities—such as the editing of the *Handbook of Latin American Studies* and the promotion of research and exchanges between Latin Americanists—are too well known to need enumeration here. The author is grateful to Dr. Howard F. Cline, Director of the Hispanic Foundation, and to his staff for their help and for having given her a chance to see some of the smoothly turning wheels of the Library of Congress. She gratefully acknowledges her debt also to Stanley L. West, former Director of Libraries of the University of Florida and former Chairman of the Farmington Plan Subcommittee on Latin American Resources, who drafted the National Acquisitions Plan for the Library of Congress. His persistence in trying to evolve a scheme that would be of help to American libraries and his refusal to be daunted by setbacks or constant redrafting command respect.

There are many others who are known to the author only through their works but who have fired her enthusiasm by their command of their subject matter and the breadth of their views. Their names stud the following pages. It is impossible to mention them all here, or all those to whom the writer is indebted for information, advice, and timely help and encouragement. She wishes, however, to express special gratitude to the following: Walter A. Hafner, for his unfailing interest; Dominick Coppola, for uncomplaining patience in answering queries, providing material and, above all, for reading the manuscript; Dr. Maurice F. Tauber, Melvil Dewey Professor of Library Service at Columbia University, for the generosity of his Foreword, and both Dr. Tauber and Mrs. Edith C. Wise, of the General University Library of New York University, for constructive criticism; Professor E. Hugh Behymer, Dean of the Graduate Library School of Long Island University, and his staff, for instruction, guidance, and encouragement; Joseph Groesbeck, Deputy Director of the Dag Hammarskjold Library, and Carlos Victor Penna, Chief of the UNESCO Division of Libraries, Documentation and Archives, for information and advice.

May this record of an exciting and thoroughly enjoyable experience give as much pleasure to others as it has given to the author.

CHAPTER I

A Glance at the Background

LACAP stands where two currents, both American, meet and mingle. One is the trend towards specialized study of foreign countries, embodied in the area studies programs evolved by the universities. The other is the trend towards cooperative acquisition, which has been evident in the United States since the nineteenth century, and particularly in the last fifty years. The second of these currents is the necessary accompaniment of the first. Given the need for knowledge, the means to obtain it had to be found. Cooperative acquisition is the tool with which American libraries have sought to solve their procurement problems and to establish bibliographic control. LACAP is only a very small part of this great sweep of events—just the top of the iceberg, as it were—but it is significant because it has its place in the wider framework—and because it works.

In order to understand LACAP's place in acquisitions from Latin America, it is necessary to look, not only at Latin America, but at library developments in the United States which involve worldwide plans, and at the place of Latin America in the world book trade.

United States interest in Latin America dates from the early days of independence. Thomas Jefferson's library, acquired by the Library of Congress in 1815, already contained a sizeable number of titles on Latin America, and in the 1860's there were exchanges of publications between the United States and five Latin American countries. This interest in Latin America has quickened in the twentieth century, when the United States has become increasingly aware of the outside world and increasingly involved with and responsible for the trend of world events. The growth of this interest is a matter of record. In a talk which he gave at the University of California, Berkeley, in 1938, Professor Manuel P. Gonzalez, Professor of Spanish Language and Literature at the University of California, Los Angeles, remarked on the

1

increase in the number of books about Latin America published
in the United States since the early 1900's, and he gave the following figures: prior to 1908, the number of titles was 46; it had
risen to 1,538 by 1938.

In his survey, *The International Exchange of Publications,*
published in 1950, Laurence J. Kipp notes the same trend. He
says:

> . . . Another source of our' need for Latin American publications is
> the number of titles published in this country about Latin America.
> . . . Since research workers and students must have publications of
> all kinds, . . . demand in the United States is growing and will con-
> tinue to grow.

Dominick Coppola, then Executive Vice-President of Stechert-
Hafner, Inc., summed up the situation in the following words in
a talk he gave in 1965 at the request of the New York Library
Association:

> One of the world's newly developing areas which has for years been
> the concern of the United States, at times critically so, is the group of
> countries to the south of us lumped together under the convenient term
> Latin America. This wide expanse, which comprises immense countries
> like Brazil and Argentina and small, but nonetheless individualistic,
> countries like El Salvador or Paraguay, has presented us for years with
> challenges, opportunities and problems second to those of no other
> world areas.
> Our country's interest in Latin America has fluctuated during the course
> of history. There have been times when we have been intensely in-
> volved, others when our concern has waned. There was a peak period
> during the Second World War which was followed by a lull. Now the
> sixties have found us intensely interested once more and there is en-
> couragingly enough, little evidence that this will subside in the near
> future.
> Dire events, such as the ones in Cuba several years ago and in the
> Dominican Republic just recently, have especially underscored the
> urgency and necessity for continued, intensive efforts to keep abreast
> of political, sociological and cultural events in those countries whose
> destinies are so closely linked with ours.

Mrs. Marietta Daniels Shepard, Associate Librarian of the

Columbus Memorial Library, dates the awakening of interest in Latin America from the First World War, which, she says in the introduction to the *Final Report* of the fifth Seminar on the Acquisition of Latin American Library Materials (SALALM), "wrenched this country from its previous state of isolated bliss." In the introduction to the *Final Report* of the previous SALALM she had already said:

> The enforced preoccupation of the United States with world events continues to be reflected in the increasing awareness on the part of the citizens of the United States of the interdependence of the peoples of the world. It has kindled an interest in the Latin American nations not only among scholars, but among businessmen, investors, and the public in general. Public and specialized libraries, as well as university and research libraries, are required to provide popular reading materials, and the photocopies of printed materials no longer available through ordinary booktrade channels.

This growing sense of the interdependence of peoples had, as a necessary counterpart, a need for information about other countries and a desire to study their history and culture, to understand their aims and motivations. New programs and new institutions sprang up in the 1920's and 1930's in order to meet these needs. The Department of State, the Library of Congress, the American Library Association, the Social Science Research Council, the American Council of Learned Societies, and great universities, such as the Universities of California, Florida and Texas, turned their attention to Latin America, among other things. The *Handbook of Latin American Studies* was launched and the Hispanic Foundation was established. Latin American area studies programs were offered by an increasing number of universities, a trend which has been accentuated by the last war and its aftermath.

But programs and institutions are not self-generating. They come about through the efforts of men and women who have the vision and courage to build for the future. Latin American studies have been fortunate in that respect. Dr. Lewis Hanke, historian and bibliographer, was the first editor of the *Handbook of Latin American Studies* and the first Director of the Hispanic Foundation. It was he who brought the *Handbook* with him when he moved to the Hispanic Foundation from Harvard, thus initiating an association that was to be permanent. Backed by a dedicated group of scholars, he laid a firm basis for the future of both the *Handbook* and the Hispanic Foundation. Other bibliographers were at work also. C. K. Jones was compiling his *Bibliography of Bibliographies of Latin America,* now going into its third edition. James B. Childs was investigating the government publications of the Latin American republics and compiling bibliographies of them. Sturgis E. Leavitt was doing the same for Latin American periodicals. J. Fred Rippy, historian of Latin America, Raul d'Eça, a future associate editor of the *Handbook,* Miron Burgin, and Francisco Aguilera, future editors, and great Latin American librarians, such as Dr. Rubens Borba de Moraes, Director of the Biblioteca Municipal de São Paulo, besides many others, helped to make the *Handbook* what it is.

They were helped by others who were more directly concerned with administration and librarianship. Marie Willis Cannon, of the Library of Congress, was particularly concerned with acquisitions. That was how she came to visit Latin America on buying trips, and to write so feelingly about the difficulties she encountered in the articles she contributed to the *Handbook*. William H. Kurth, then of the Order Division of the Library of Congress, was to follow in her footsteps when he made his trip for the Cooperative Library Mission, about which more will be said later. In a wider sphere, important librarians like Archibald MacLeish and Luther H. Evans, both Librarians of Congress before being called to higher posts, one as Assistant Secretary of State and the other as Director-General of UNESCO, and Arthur E. Gropp, Librarian of the Columbus Memorial Library, helped to push the frontiers of knowledge forward. At the same time, other librarians were thinking in the direction of cooperative acquisitions on a world scale. Such men as Keyes D. Metcalf, international library consultant and the first Chairman of the Farmington Plan Committee, Edwin E. Williams, of the Harvard University Library, Verner W. Clapp, library specialist and consultant, Julian P. Boyd, Librarian of Princeton, and MacLeish himself, were all turning their thoughts in that direction. When MacLeish became Assistant Secretary of State, he was in a position to give effect to this thinking. The Farmington Plan was the result, and it too was to have an impact on acquisitions from Latin America. The trend was to be towards planned cooperative acquisition and a division of responsibility for collecting from different areas.[1]

LACAP was therefore a latecomer in a field where giants had walked before. Cooperative acquisition in itself is not a new idea. It goes back to Alexandre Vattemare (in the 1840's) and, among librarians, to Charles Coffin Jewett (1850) and Justin Winsor (1876). However, the scale of the present efforts is unprecedented. The Farmington Plan, the largest cooperative acquisitions scheme ever undertaken by American or any other libraries, is worldwide. Its aim is described as follows in the 1961 *Farmington Plan Handbook:*

> . . . [To]make sure that one copy at least of each new foreign publica-
> tion that might reasonably be expected to interest a research worker
> in the United States would be acquired by an American library, prompt-
> ly listed in the National Union Catalog, and made available by inter-
> library loan or photographic reproduction.

The principle of "complete coverage"—or, more accurately, "systematic coverage"—has been so fully accepted in the United States that in his article on storage and deposit libraries in the November, 1960, issue of *College and Research Libraries,* Dr. Jerrold Orne, Librarian of the University of North Carolina, could speak of the need for a "nation-wide plan to acquire the entire output of world printing on a single copy basis," and say that such a plan involved "complete understanding and accept-ance of the national responsibility for acquisition, on a global basis, of the printed record."

The provision of library materials in increasing quantities is a necessity which must be met if the universities of the future—even ten years from now—are to provide the services required of them as a result of the population and knowledge explosions. The following figures, which were given at the Twentieth Annual Na-tional Conference on Higher Education in March, 1965, give some idea of the dimensions of the problem. Over the five years following 1965, more students will be added to the enrollment of American colleges and universities than were enrolled in the whole of 1954, and the average size of each institution, which in-creased by 55 per cent between 1955 and 1960, will increase by

another 50 per cent before 1970. The production of knowledge
doubles every ten years; there is a hundred times as much to know
now as there was in 1900, and there will be a thousand times more
by the year 2,000.

The trend is further accentuated by the tremendous growth in
scientific publishing. The International Federation of Library
Associations (IFLA) found the situation disquieting in 1963,
when it gave the following cry of alarm in *Libraries in the World:*

> Some 330,000 book titles were published in 1959 . . . ; more than
> 80,000 periodicals bring three million articles to the notice of a dum-
> founded world, and this figure does not include 30,000 newspapers.
> . . . Still more staggering than these figures is the knowledge that the
> quantity of scientific literature yearly published is growing so rapidly
> that it doubles every five years.

The Library of Congress is feeling the same pressure. According to the *Library of Congress Information Bulletin* of September
7, 1965, the growing interest of Congress in matters connected
with the Hispanic countries in fiscal 1965 caused a minor "research explosion" in the research and reference work of the Hispanic Law Division. The *Bulletin* adds:

> . . . This interest was sparked not only by events in the hemisphere
> but also by increasingly closer ties of the United States and its neigh-
> bors through cooperative programs in the economic, social and political
> fields.

The Alliance for Progress and the programs of the Organization
of American States (OAS) are outstanding examples of such cooperation.

It is obvious that the time for piecemeal methods is past. What
librarians must now consider is how to obtain materials in quan-
tity. If the aim is to acquire at least one copy of every publication
which might conceivably interest some future research worker, it
can be achieved only through a cooperative acquisitions procedure, and only if universities are willing to provide book budgets large enough to enable their libraries to participate in cooperative schemes. The financial implications of such schemes
cannot be light. It would seem that they can be accepted only by

the institutions of an affluent society. Nevertheless, the government of the United Kingdom—always careful with public funds—has now established five new Centres (*sic*) of Latin American Studies on the recommendation of the Committee on Latin American Studies, which also recommended LACAP to the attention of British librarians.

Compared with the Farmington Plan, LACAP is a modest scheme. It covers only one continent and it does not aim at acquiring the entire output of Latin American printing. Nevertheless, by the magnitude of its aim—the acquisition of all current imprints on a multiple-copy basis—it is in harmony with the thinking behind the Farmington Plan. It therefore has its place within the framework of the larger national schemes, and it reflects the spirit of the times in which it was born.

CHAPTER II

Latin America in the World Book Trade

It is impossible to disagree with the following statement, made by R. E. Barker in *Books for All,* the study of the world book trade he carried out for the United Nations Educational, Scientific and Cultural Organization (UNESCO), which was published in 1956:

> To trace the intricate pattern of world trade in books with reasonable accuracy complete and reliable statistics are required. A difficulty which has arisen in writing this study, however, is that statistics in the book trade, as in many other branches of commerce, are often inadequate. There is, for example, no universal standard definition of a book, because many countries do not distinguish between what constitutes a book or a pamphlet; others lump books with unknown quantities of other kinds of printed matter; others, again, exclude postal exports and consignments below certain values which play an extremely important part in the general exchange of books.

When *Books for All* was published, the only definition of a

book with any semblance of universal applicability was that
recommended by the UNESCO Conference on the Improvement
of Bibliographical Services in 1950, i.e., "a non-periodical literary
publication containing 49 or more pages, not counting the covers."
A pamphlet was defined as "a non-periodical publication containing between 5 and 48 pages, not counting the covers." Discussions
continued for more than ten years before definitions were finally
recommended by the thirteenth session of the UNESCO General
Conference, in November, 1964. These definitions, which are
used in this book, are as follows:

> A book is a non-periodical publication of at least 49 pages, exclusive
> of the cover pages, published in the country (*sic*) and made available
> to the public.
> A pamphlet is a non-periodical publication of at least 5 but not more
> than 48 pages, exclusive of the cover pages, published in a particular
> country and made available to the public.

The problem of statistics is not solved, however, by the adoption
of a definition, unless it is generally applied in statistical reporting, which is far from being the case. As is pointed out in the
UNESCO publication *Basic Facts and Figures* for 1961, the statistics of book production are not necessarily an exact reflection
of the national book market, in any event, because some countries
export much of their production and others import to meet their
needs. Moreover, as the statistical unit of book production is a
"title," statistics rarely show the actual output, i.e., the total number of volumes printed in a country. Barker sets against this defect
"the fact that statistics based on titles do illustrate the variety of
books produced in individual countries throughout the world."
A further difficulty arises in connection with the nature of the
publication the title represents. In the statistics published by
UNESCO and in the *United Nations Statistical Yearbook* each
title is counted as a unit but, unless otherwise stated, the figures
cover "all non-periodical publications, including pamphlets, first
editions of originals and (new) translations, re-editions and the
more important government reports." These statistics are, therefore, in no way comparable with those of LACAP. The LACAP
titles are those of monographs by Latin American authors, published and sold in Latin America. They include both books and

pamphlets as defined by UNESCO but they exclude translations, textbooks, juvenile literature, reprints, microfilms, sound recordings, and periodicals.

Although the figures are only approximate and not strictly comparable, it nevertheless seems worthwhile to attempt a rough assessment of the position of Latin America in the world book trade. In *Basic Facts and Figures* for 1958, UNESCO estimates the world book production of 1957 as "probably between 310,000 and 320,000 titles," of which Latin America accounted for some 9,000 titles, or 3 per cent. The figures for 1958, 1959, and 1960 given in the subsequent annual issues of the same publication are 320,000-330,000 in 1958, "probably 330,000" in 1959, and "probably about 340,000" in 1960. Latin American book production for the same years is given as 10,000 or 3 per cent (1958), 12,000 or 4 per cent (1959), and 13,000—again 4 per cent—in 1960.

These percentages seem to be in line with Barker's analysis of book production figures by language groups. His total of 100 per cent covers only the books published in nine languages—English, Russian, German, Japanese, French, Spanish, Italian, Portuguese, and Chinese—and his figures are not all for the same years and do not cover all the countries of Latin America. Some of them— those for Argentina, Brazil, and Spain, for instance—relate to the whole three-year period 1952-1954, but the only figures for Nicaragua and the Dominican Republic are for 1947 and 1949 respectively, and many Latin American countries are omitted. On the basis of the figures at his disposal for Spain and nine Latin American countries—Argentina, Brazil, Cuba, the Dominican Republic, Guatemala, Honduras, Nicaragua, Panama, and Peru—Barker gives the following breakdown of Spanish-language book production:

Spain	3,445
Argentina	3,600
Other Latin American countries	4,000
TOTAL	11,045

The figure of 11,045 represents 7.5 per cent of the total production in the nine languages considered. Barker notes that the figure of 4,000 for "Other Latin American countries" is "probably an underestimate; actual figures are unavailable in most cases." If the production of Spain, which is just under one-third of the total for the Spanish-speaking countries, is deducted, the figure for the production of Latin America is a little over 5 per cent. The UNESCO figure of 4 per cent for the part of Latin America in world book production would therefore seem to be a reasonable estimate.

The figures given in the UNESCO publications *Basic Facts and Figures* (up to 1960) and the *UNESCO Statistical Yearbook* (from 1961 onwards) are virtually identical with the book production figures given in the *United Nations Statistical Yearbook,* although there are some slight differences. UNESCO is the source of the figures given by Eustasio Antonio García in *Desarrollo de la industria editorial argentina,* and both UNESCO and the United Nations are quoted as sources in the *Bowker Annual of Library and Booktrade Information,* from which the following table has been compiled. It shows the book production figures from 1955 to 1964. The United States is included as a standard of comparison.

TABLE 1

United States and Latin American Book Production, 1955-1964*

Country	1955	1956	1957	1958	1959	1960	1961a	1962	1963	1964
Argentina	2,617	2,435	2,530	2,623	3,701	4,063	3,703	3,323	3,989	3,319
Bolivia			71							
Brazil	3,385	4,247	4,659	4,911	5,337				5,133	
Chile	1,866	1,498	1,534	1,028	1,227	1,518	1,389	1,040		1,577
Colombia	438		317							
Cuba			467			394	698			
Dominican Republic			136						71	
Ecuador				61						
Guatemala			105		288	235	207	500	90	
Haiti				19						39
Honduras		91						189		
Mexico	923				2,500b	1,964	2,674	3,760	4,362	4,661
Nicaragua										
Panama										
Paraguay				30						
Peru			506	587	583	653		791		946
United States			13,142	13,462	14,876c	15,012c	18,060	21,901	25,784	28,451
Uruguay	66	104					266	217	140	194
Venezuela	538	317					338		743	

Source: UNESCO. Figures include both books and pamphlets.

a Source for 1961 figures: *United Nations Statistical Yearbook 1962*, pp. 641-645.

b Provisional or estimated data.

c These figures refer only to the production of the book trade (commercial publishing) and omit a large part of total book production, such as government and university publications, etc.

* These figures are taken from the *Bowker Annual of Library and Booktrade Information*, 1964, 1965, and 1966. They are reproduced here with the permission of the R. R. Bowker Company.

It can be seen that the information on book production is extremely patchy, and that something more is needed to form an accurate idea of Latin American book production. The need for more accurate data led the delegates to the Primer Congreso Iberoamericano de Asociaciones y Cámeras del Libro, held in Mexico City from May 19-23, 1964, to recommend that funds should be sought to make a statistical study of the book industry in the Spanish-Portuguese language area. Until fresh data are forthcoming, however, existing figures must be used.

One source of book production statistics is the work done by Peter S. Jennison and William H. Kurth. For their study, *Books in the Americas,* they tapped every possible source of information, including the Hispanic Foundation of the Library of Congress, the Columbus Memorial Library, the Division of American Republics of the U. S. Bureau of Foreign Commerce, and the bibliographical institutions and publications of the countries themselves, and each figure is carefully documented.

Writing in 1959, the authors give the total book production of the western hemisphere as between 25,000 and 30,000 titles annually, divided according to languages as follows:

English (U. S. and Canada)	14,000
Spanish	7,000
Portuguese	4,000
French (Canada and Haiti)	500
TOTAL	25,500

Barker's estimate of 7,600 for Spanish American book production was therefore close to the mark.

Regarding the availability of data, Jennison and Kurth make the following comment:

In most instances, no firm data are readily available; the figures are in some cases outdated, or where estimates are given, their reliability is somewhat suspect. But if these figures are used as indicators rather than as precise statements, they serve an illustrative purpose and provide approximate quantitative information with respect to the nature and scope of book publication in the area. Yet it is necessary to know first —more exactly than is presently possible—what the national book production totals are, and to have these facts related to a set of agreed-upon norms and definitions. This very lack of solid information—how many books are published, how many pamphlets, translations, reprints, etc., — itself constitutes an impediment to measuring the status of book production in the Americas . . .

Jennison and Kurth point out also a number of other factors which must be taken into account when the figures are considered: first, the lack of a common definition of a "book;" secondly, the use of the word *edición* to designate both a reprint and a revised edition of a book; thirdly, the inclusion, in the statistics reported, of commercial, government, and privately printed publications, and also translations and textbooks. These figures nevertheless give some idea of the book production situation as it was at the time of the fourth SALALM (1959) and just prior to the launching of LACAP (1960). The figures are as follows:

TABLE 2

Book Production in the Americas*

Country	Books	Year
Argentina	2,560	1957
Bolivia	100e	1957
Brazil	3,235	1956
Canada	1,094	1957
Chile	747	1957
Colombia	438	1955
Costa Rica	25e	1958
Cuba	467	1957
Dominican Republic	136	1957
Ecuador	70e	1958
El Salvador	25e	1957
Guatemala	105	1957
Haiti	31	1955
Honduras	91	1956
Mexico	923	1955
Nicaragua	30e	1958
Panama	50e	1958
Paraguay	30e	1958
Peru	507	1957
United States	13,142	1957
Uruguay	65	1955
Venezuela	538	1955
TOTAL	24,409	

e Estimate.

* Reproduced from Jennison and Kurth, *Books in the Americas*, p. 21, with the permission of the Pan American Union.

A comparison of tables 1 and 2 shows that the figures are almost identical, except for Brazil and Chile. The difference is not easy to explain in either case, for the data from which the figures for the two countries are derived are the same for both tables: 2,366 books and 1,861 pamphlets for Brazil, and 695 books and 838 pamphlets for Chile. The figure for Chile in table 2 would appear to represent books only.

As there is virtually no difference between the two sets of figures, it is permissible to conclude that they may be taken as a reasonably accurate basis. Before greater accuracy can be achieved, there must be some improvement in statistical reporting. In the meantime, the figures in the *Bowker Annual* can be accepted, bearing in mind that "no firm data are readily available," and that "if these figures are used as indicators rather than as precise statements, they serve an illustrative purpose."

The peculiarities of the Latin American book trade are discussed in chapter III. It must be pointed out here, however, that the private printing and distribution of authors' works, the lack of reliable and up-to-date bibliographies in many areas, and the absence of imprints from the provinces in the book trade of the large cities must have a distorting effect on the statistics of book production. The improvement in procurement effected by LACAP may, by increasing the flow of books to the centers of the book trade, contribute indirectly to the improvement of book production statistics.

CHAPTER III

Special Characteristics of the Latin American Book Trade

The organization of the Seminars on the Acquisition of Latin American Library Materials concentrated attention on the difficulties inherent in the Latin American book trade and brought them sharply into focus. The theme of the first Seminar (1956), as enunciated by Dr. A. Curtis Wilgus, Director of the School of Inter-American Studies of the University of Florida, was "to consider the problems involved in finding, buying, and controlling library matters relating to Latin America." The trips to Latin America made by Marie Willis Cannon and William Kurth in the 1940's and 1950's helped to increase knowledge of the problems without providing a solution for them. It was not until Dr. Nettie Lee Benson, Head of the Latin American Collection of the University of Texas, visited four Latin American countries on behalf of LACAP in 1960 that real progress with actual acquisitions was made. Her trip was the spearhead of an attack on the problems which has completely changed the picture of book procurement from Latin America.

Before discussing the problems of the book trade itself, some consideration must be given to the political and economic framework in which it functions. Most of the countries of Latin America are still under-developed—or still in process of development—and many of them are dependent for their economic well-being on the export of a single product, such as tin, oil, or coffee. Although great efforts have been made in recent years to diversify the economies of these countries, they are still profoundly affected by fluctuations in the prices of a few commodities on the world markets, and their economic vulnerability has contributed to the political instability of the area as a whole.

In a preliminary report entitled "The Acquisition of Research Materials from South America,"[1] Kurth had the following to say on this point in 1959:

> Two conditions may be cited which profoundly affect the production of research materials. These are political and economic factors, which may often be interrelated. They are basic because the political and economic factors are subject to wider and deeper fluctuations than in the U. S., and the implication on research materials is naturally closely linked to these factors.

He goes on to discuss the case of Argentina, where, he was informed, the annual output of about 5,000 titles in the early 1950's had declined to less than half by 1958 owing to a number of factors, "among them outside competition, and worsening economic conditions which have resulted in a reduction of capital for publishing activities." He continues:

The leading commodities of the South American republics and their economic success or failure on the world's markets relate importantly to the book industry. Thus, in a real sense, such commodities as lead, zinc, coffee, tin, and oil, and their marketability and price exert a strong influence on what and how much is published. Dollar shortages direct imports to commodities regarded as essential; import duties on certain commodities necessary to book production may be set relatively high.

One of the commodities necessary to the book trade is paper. In *Books in Latin America*, a study carried out for Franklin Publications in 1961, Francisco Aguilera (Hispanic Foundation, Library of Congress) , Curtis Benjamin (McGraw Hill Book Company) , and Dan Lacy (American Book Publishers Council) say:

> In every Latin American country, the high cost of book paper in relation to book prices is a serious problem. In all countries except Mexico, domestically produced (or "national") book papers are of inferior quality, or in short supply, or both.
> While the problem of quality, cost and supply of book papers is acute in all countries, it varies in pattern and degree from country to country.

Writing in 1961, the authors of the study pointed out that there were certain traits which were common to the situation in many of the countries studied. In Brazil, Argentina, and Colombia, locally produced paper was expensive and usually of poor quality. Peru did not produce any paper and Colombia so little that both countries were dependent on imports from the sterling and dollar areas and therefore had a foreign exchange problem. Argentina and Mexico imposed duties on imported paper, but Mexico allowed a rebate if more than 60 per cent of the books for which the paper was to be used were to be exported. In *La edición de libros en Argentina,* Raúl H. Bottaro says that the Comisión para la Promoción del Libro Argentino tried to get the duty lifted in 1962, but the Ministry of Economy was obdurate. Further restrictions were imposed in 1965.

Juan Carlos De Carli comments rather acidly on the efforts of the Comisión para la Promoción del Libro Argentino in a talk which he gave at the Fundación Interamericana de Bibliotecología Franklin, Buenos Aires, in 1965:

Se dice que la liberación de ingreso de papeles y demás materias primas constituye la panacea para los males del libro; pero no se habla del uso racional de tipos y calidades de papeles, porque cada cual obra según *su* propio criterio y *su* propia experiencia.

[People say that the removal of the duties on paper and other raw materials is a panacea for the ills of the book trade; but no one says anything about the proper use of kinds and grades of paper, for everyone acts as *he* sees fit, on the basis of *his* experience.]

It can be seen that De Carli, too, is in favor of cooperation.

So much has been said and written about the special characteristics of the Latin American book trade since the first SALALM was held, in 1956, that Robert Vosper, then Director of Libraries of the University of Kansas, could no longer say today, as he did in the April, 1955, issue of *Library Trends,* that "the literature on the subject is thin or non-existent." There is now so much information on the subject that it is difficult to formulate the characteristics succinctly. The SALALM records contain an immense amount of data on all aspects of the Latin American book trade, and to them must be added Kurth's detailed account of the Cooperative Library Mission to Latin America, and innumerable articles written by such authorities as T. R. Barcus and Verner W. Clapp, Marie Willis Cannon, Howard F. Cline, Peter de la Garza, Marietta Daniels Shepard, Stanley L. West, and Edwin E. Williams.

The persons connected with LACAP, particularly Dr. Benson and Dominick Coppola, have contributed largely to the pool of knowledge. The difficulties sketched in by Coppola in the paper which he submitted to the first Seminar were pointed up by Dr. Benson's reports to the fifth and sixth Seminars, and by Coppola's exultant "Breakthrough in Latin American Acquisitions," which was submitted to the seventh Seminar. More recently—in April, 1966—Coppola summarized the factors affecting the book trade in Latin America in a talk he gave at Columbia University. This has been used as the basis for the present account.

Organization of the Latin American Book Trade

The book trade is struggling or disorganized in all the Latin American countries except Mexico and Argentina, and nowhere is it organized as it is in Europe or the United States. What would

be called "vanity printing" in the United States does not bear the
same stigma in Latin America; except in the big publishing
centers, such as Buenos Aires, Mexico City and Brazil, most of the
works written by Latin American authors are privately printed
and distributed. The *editoriales* are often no more than contract
printers. They frequently deliver the entire printing to the author
and keep no record of the titles they have printed.

This is brought out very clearly in Dr. Benson's report to the
fifth Seminar. The Casa de la Cultura Ecuatoriana—the most
active booksellers in Ecuador—sent a circular to all the printers
in Quito asking them to give the titles of all books published in
1958 and 1959, but the results were not quite what had been
expected. They are best described in Dr. Benson's own words:

> . . . Only three or four printers supplied any titles and practically all
> who replied stated that they kept no record of the titles of books they
> had published. If you found the printer's shop, you could not learn the
> address of the author. And many times the printing shop could not be
> located for the simple reason that it is not at all uncommon for the
> author . . . to require the shop to give as the name of the printing
> establishment some name that he has dreamed up, or not to give the
> name of the printer at all. It is impossible therefore to try to buy the
> books by making contacts (*sic*) [contracts?] with the printers or publish-
> ers. They print. They do not distribute.

Dr. Benson adds that even when there are publishers in the
American sense—and some do exist in the four countries (Ecuador,
Peru, Chile, and Bolivia) she visited in 1960—"one is surprised to
find that they do not distribute all the books they publish. They
too print for authors who carry the whole stock home for distribution as they see fit." These are not, as might be supposed,
insignificant works by little known authors, according to Dr.
Benson. She says that although the publishers sometimes had in
stock a few copies of a work printed by them for an author, they
did not count it as one of their imprints; they were simply handling a few copies for the author.

Dr. Benson estimates that 50 to 75 per cent of all books published in the countries she viisted in 1960 were not distributed
by publishers, and that in Ecuador and Bolivia the percentage was
even higher. Stanley L. West, until recently Director of Libraries

of the University of Florida and Chairman of the Farmington Plan Subcommittee on Latin American resources, reported to the Association of Research Libraries (ARL) in 1961 that only 10 per cent of Latin American book production found its way into normal commercial channels.

The custom of an author distributing his own works is radically different from United States business practice. In her report to the fifth Seminar Dr. Benson describes how the author deposits a few copies with one or more booksellers—often without leaving his address—and makes an agreement to tell his friends so they will go there and perhaps buy other books at the same time. The frustrating results of this practice are described as follows:

> In one case . . . only a few copies of a desirable title were left. I asked for all of them and was told that I could have them. The next day . . . I was told that the author did not wish to sell all the remaining copies because . . . he did not want [his friends] disappointed when they did come by. . . . . On another occasion a bookstore did not have enough copies, and when it contacted the author to get more copies, the author wanted to know to whom they were to be sold and raised the price of them.

She adds that in Santiago, Chile, a book dealer told her some good authors did not distribute their books to bookstores at all but gave them to their friends or tried to sell them to individuals.

Another difference from United States practice is the amount and type of printing done by government and semi-government agencies. The range of this type of printing is much wider than in the United States, and it includes, besides the usual official publications, important works in the fields of literature, linguistics, fine arts, and the social sciences. Kurth gives an example of this in his Preliminary Report:

> The Banco de la República, in Colombia, not a government agency but analogous to the Federal Reserve System in the U. S., published in 1958 a translation into Spanish of Sophocles as well as other fine publications in various subject fields.

Dr. Benson estimates that possibly one-fourth of the book production of Latin America falls into this category of publicly printed material, and she describes the headaches involved in purchasing it. The difficulty with this type of publication and those of university presses is that, even when they can be located, they cannot usually be bought. They are intended only for gift or exchange, or in the case of a university professor, they may be turned over to the author for distribution. In the latter case, the problems are exactly the same as for private commercial printing. In the former, the difficulties, although different, are equally frustrating—difficulty in finding acceptable material for exchange, lack of money for wrapping and mailing, lack of staff time, etc.

According to Coppola, booksellers in Latin America show little interest, as a rule, in promoting the sale of books by local authors. Because of the small margin of profit on Latin American works, booksellers tend to concentrate on the sale of imported books— from France, Germany, and the United States, for instance— which are bigger money-makers. This tendency is encouraged by the fact that it is easier for booksellers to obtain translations of American books under certain United States programs—those of Franklin Publications and the United States Information Agency, for instance—than to obtain the works of their own national authors.

In an article published March, 1958, in *Publishers Weekly,* S. W. Wasley says the selling price of a locally produced book can be anywhere from 40 (Cuba) to 400 (Brazil) per cent lower than that of an imported U. S. book. Dr. Benson describes the bookstores in Santiago, Chile, as being stocked, not with Chilean books, but with the very latest foreign books, among which there may be possibly half-a-dozen Chilean titles. Thus the bookstores are full of materials that American libraries do not want—translations, children's books, textbooks—and the books by local authors, which the American libraries would like to have, are hard to find.

Works by national authors have to be tracked down, not only in bookstores but in news stands, stationery shops, and even toy-shops. In one of his letters from Managua, Nicaragua, Coppola laments the fact that shops where he hoped to find books carried more stationery than books. Guillermo Baraya Borda, the LACAP agent, writing from San Salvador, says "I think the meaning of *librería* is different in Central America because they sell gifts and toys instead of books." A further difficulty in Central America particularly is that the situation changes with great rapidity. Writing about a bookstore in Costa Rica, Coppola says, "[It] used to carry some worthwhile books but is actually now a stationery store."

About Guatemala City he writes, "I had envisioned a wealth of bookstores but I should have known better," and he adds:

> . . . Bookstores disappear, change hands, change addresses, change activities. "Eichenberger" was a name recollected as someone we used to rely on—now it is a shop selling only giftware and photographic supplies. Not one book. "Sanchez de Guise" used to be important especially as a publisher. Now there is an . . . old lady who is struggling to sell some of the old stock and stationery as well.

The hazards are not only commercial. One man, who had supplied material to Stechert-Hafner in the past and who also ran the local geographical and historical society, had been ambushed three years before and nearly lost his life. He did lose a leg and subsequently gave up being active, as well he might.

The above examples are all from Central America, but numerous others are cited by Baraya from the Caribbean, and the necessity of tracking down books is constantly mentioned by Dr. Benson in her reports from South America proper.

As booksellers are not interested in promoting the sale of works by Latin American authors, they do not trouble to display locally published books. Anyone who wishes to buy them must seek them out, not only in the different bookstores but even in the bookstores that carry them. Describing the situation in Santiago, Chile, in 1960, Dr. Benson says in her report to the fifth Seminar:

> . . . If someone inquires about a Chilean title, more often than not, it is found down low behind a counter, behind a door, in some drawer or far toward the back of the store. National titles are very seldom prominently displayed unless they are published in some foreign country. More often than not, the store does not know what the titles are and could [not] care less. If you want to know what is available, it is up to you to look for yourself.

Titles Are Soon Out of Print

In Latin America, titles go out of print very quickly, often after a year or two and sometimes almost immediately, owing to small printings. Dr. Benson reported in 1960 that the reason for the small printings in Ecuador, Chile, Peru, and Bolivia was that booksellers were not interested in selling books by national authors. She added that the better publishers did not seem to have much confidence in their product and therefore issued small editions, and the authors who had their books printed also necessarily had very limited editions printed. Jennison and Kurth give approximate figures for Bolivia in *Books in the Americas:* an edition of a scholarly work in the humanities would run to about 1,000 to 2,000 copies; editions of works in the field of law and jurisprudence would be from 1,000 to 3,000. The figures given by Bottaro in *La edición de libros en Argentina* are much higher, as is to be expected from a country with a flourishing publishing industry, but they include, not only textbooks, reference books, and children's books, but radio and film scripts. He gives 7,400 and 10,000 for the average number of copies printed in 1958 and 1960 respectively.

In his talk at Columbia University, Coppola said that the lack of an appreciable Latin American library market and the fact that there was no sizeable reading public were factors which made for small printings. He added:

> . . . And when publishers are undercapitalized, as they usually are, the lack of any appreciable demand is a decisive factor which not only influences how many copies of a title should be printed but also determines whether a title should be printed at all.

The lack of a library market is emphasized by the authors of *Books in Latin America* also. Writing in 1961, they say:

> . . . One market that is sorely missed by the Latin American publisher is the sustaining *library or "institutional" market.* This institutional market, such as it is, is difficult and costly to reach within each country, and much more so from one Latin American country to another. Thus the Latin American publisher . . . does not have a ready-made and available basic market for certain support of first editions of books of many types.

The market is still further reduced by illiteracy. In *Books in Latin America* it is estimated that, owing to illiteracy, only one-third of the Spanish-language population could make "minimally effective use" of books in Spanish, and the effective market is further reduced by poverty and the inaccessibility of books in rural areas. Thus, according to the authors, the book market is in fact restricted to the well educated, moderately well-off urban residents, of whom there are far fewer, in relation to the total Spanish-speaking population, than there are in relation to the total population in the United States or Western Europe. They add that textbook publishing is the only really profitable venture, and even these markets are small by comparison with the United States and Europe.

It would be a mistake, however, to assume that when a Latin American bookseller says that a title is *agotado,* it is really out of print. He usually means it is out of stock in his store. There may be several copies of it in a store half a block away, but the bookseller will not go and look for them. "Out of stock" very soon becomes synonymous with "out of print," however, because the few copies in the store down the street soon disappear, and they are not replaced as the whole printing is very small. The author may have more copies in a trunk under his bed, but if the potential purchaser cannot find him, the title is for all practical purposes out of print. It is essential to buy new titles as soon as they appear if they are to be bought at all. If LACAP has succeeded, it is partly because this necessity was understood from the very beginning.

Lack of Bibliographical Information and Difficulties of Communication

The lack of bibliographies and indexes is a recurrent theme in the SALALM discussions of procurement from Latin America. Not all the participants found the situation uniformly bleak, however, and there was at least one dissenting voice in the chorus of lamentation. In a paper he submitted to the fifth Seminar, in 1960, Nathan L. Haverstock, then the editor of the *Handbook of Latin American Studies,* maintained that the bibliographical information available was not fully used. The situation has improved considerably over the last ten years, owing to national efforts and the work done by UNESCO, the Library of Congress, the OAS, SALALM, the R. R. Bowker Company, and various groups and individuals, including LACAP. In 1956, however, when the first SALALM was held, American librarians had to rely mainly on the *Handbook of Latin American Studies,* supplemented by the monthly accessions lists of the Columbus Memorial Library and whatever partial bibliographies, publishers' lists and booksellers' catalogs they could obtain. The *Handbook,* although a most admirable and scholarly work, does not appear until a year later than the current imprints that it lists, and for a number of years it appeared with some delay, although this has not been the case for some time. In any event, current titles listed in the *Handbook* may be out of print before they can be ordered.

Coppola pointed out in his talk at Columbia that local bibliographies appear far too late, with the result that a book may be out of print before it can be ordered. It was noted at the ninth Seminar, held in June, 1964, that the *Anuario bibliográfico Peruano* was up to only 1957, and Enid Baa, then Librarian of the Caribbean Organization, commented on the late appearance of three Caribbean bibliographies in the working paper which she submitted to the eighth Seminar.

A further difficulty pointed out by Coppola is that publishers' lists, flyers and catalogs do not usually differentiate between native and foreign authors. It is therefore almost impossible, except in obvious cases, to distinguish the works of national authors from translations and reprints of foreign works.

The barriers of communication and transportation within each country are often formidable. In vast areas of Argentina there are almost no roads, and the usual means of communication is the horse. Similar conditions prevail in many of the other Latin American republics. There is not only a lack of physical access to the more remote areas of such countries as Brazil, Colombia, and Argentina, but a lack of knowledge about what goes on there. Dr. Benson found that some bookstores in Bogotá which had branches in all the other nine large cities of Colombia—where, she says, a number of good titles are published annually—not only did not have copies of all those titles but did not even know that some of them existed. She sums up the situation as follows:

> . . . It should be remembered that the book dealers and distributors in the capitals find the problem of getting imprints from the interior of the country even more difficult than we find getting them from the capitals. It is easier and more profitable for them to get books from

the U. S. or Europe or Mexico than it is to get them from the interior of their country. Actually, in many cases, communications between the capitals of different countries is faster and easier than communications between the capital and the interior of the country. Even in Argentina, I have been told . . . that the only way [to get books from outside Buenos Aires] is to . . . check personally and buy on the spot. This is expensive and is not a paying proposition if you have sales for only a few copies.

This is one of the areas to which LACAP has paid special attention. The LACAP representatives have made a point of becoming thoroughly acquainted with the local scene in each country, visiting not only the capital cities but also the out-of-the-way centers. To mention only a few examples, Dr. Benson visited Cuzco and Arequipa as well as Lima when she was in Peru in 1960, and Guayaquil as well as Quito in Ecuador. Felipe García Beraza, Director of the Centro Mexicano de Escritores, made a trip for LACAP in 1961 which took in Cholula, Puebla, Orizaba, Córdoba, Jalapa, Veracruz, Coatepec, and Tlacotalpan. Baraya made two trips inside Colombia in 1962 and 1963, visiting Tunja, Cartagena, Barranquilla, and Santa Marta on the first trip, and Cali, Popayán and Medellín on the second.

The Attitude of Latin American Book Dealers to Export Orders

Dealing with the Latin American book trade is one of the most frustrating experiences for a librarian accustomed to American business methods. In the paper which she submitted to the first Seminar, Mrs. Emma Crosland Simonson, then of the General Library, University of California, Berkeley, stresses the need for an approach which is different from the usual American business practice. She points out that for Latin American firms, business is not just business. Business relations must be established on a personal basis if material is to be received successfully, rapidly, and consistently. She recommends various ways of achieving and maintaining personal contact, which include exchanges of personnel, on-the-spot purchases by visiting professors, sending a Spanish and/or Portuguese speaking library staff member to the area, and letting the firms know not only the libraries' needs but their "excellencies." On the last point, she says:

. . . Many do not have a definite idea of our interest in their culture, nor the extent of concentrated study being done in the United States on Latin America. One firm asked "Why so many books on Argentine poetry?" When he learned the number of courses offered in Latin American literature, the number of professors in the Spanish and Portuguese Department, and the fact that the university has on its faculty one of the leading authorities on their literature, his attitude changed, and he was willing to cut the red tape Perón had set up for so much shipping to foreign markets.

The importance of using the local language, whether in correspondence or in conversation with Latin American booksellers, was recognized by thoughtful librarians before the Seminars were organized. Writing in *Serial Slants* in July, 1953, Dr. Benson makes a point which is valid not only for serials but for all publications from Latin America. She points out that correspondence in Spanish "pays off in better service and better understanding," and Latin American businessmen "put more emphasis on how they obtain their financial returns than on the amount of the returns involved." She adds:

. . . They are interested, of course in the financial end; but . . . they are as a rule more interested in the personal factors involved—in becoming better acquainted with whom they are doing business, knowing that their product or service is really valued and appreciated. . . . This explains why many Latin American book dealers refuse to have any mail order business. To do so in their opinion deprives them of the primary benefits of any business venture—the personal social relations with their customer.

The use of a bilingual form letter was recommended by Kurth in a paper submitted to the second Seminar, and also in his report on the Cooperative Library Mission. The use of Spanish is one of the basic principles of the LACAP operation. Coppola speaks Spanish fluently, Dr. Benson has a mastery of the language, and it is Baraya's native tongue.

But even correspondence in Spanish will not interest Latin American book dealers in small orders, which they consider a nuisance. In "LACAP Report No. 2," submitted to the sixth Seminar, Dr. Benson recounts how a dealer in Buenos Aires told her "they received many orders from libraries which they simply threw in the wastebasket." One dealer showed her a long list of orders for one, two, or even as many as five titles, and told her it was just not worth his while to send those few items; "hence he threw the orders into the trash." Another dealer said the same thing and added that mailing and invoicing were too costly when the order was for only one copy of a few titles.

One of the great advantages of LACAP orders to dealers in Latin America is precisely that the number of copies is large enough to offset the trouble and cost of shipping. But there are several dealers in Buenos Aires who are not interested in orders for less than a hundred copies at a time, so even LACAP fails to score with them.

Government regulations are another complicating factor. The 1955 edition of the UNESCO publication, *Trade Barriers to Knowledge*, mentions only three Latin American countries which require registration or licensing for exports of books—Colombia, Mexico, and Peru. Jennison and Kurth found that export duties, registration, or licensing were required in Bolivia, Brazil, Chile, Colombia, Costa Rica, Ecuador, and Nicaragua in 1958. Only in three cases do they state unequivocally that there are no export formalities—in Argentina, El Salvador and Venezuela. The situation is apt to change at short notice. For instance, Argentina imposed restrictions on exports in 1965 which have seriously hampered the dispatch of books from that country. According to Francisco García Cambeiro, a bookseller from Buenos Aires who participated in the eleventh Seminar, dealers who seek to evade the regulations risk imprisonment. The Seminar adopted a resolution expressing its concern to the Argentine Embassy.

When the Latin American book dealer is not tied up in the red tape of export regulations, he often runs into other difficulties, which are largely financial. Shipments are expensive to handle, and he does not usually receive payment for them until they have arrived at their destination, which may take several months. When he is paid, it is neither easy nor cheap for him to cash the check he receives because of the exchange control procedures. Time and again Dr. Benson was obliged to pay cash in order to induce booksellers to ship the books she had selected. Often she was obliged to wrap and mail them herself. As the payments pro--

cedures of many libraries preclude the possibility of advance payments—which Baraya feels to be undesirable in principle—the
problem seems to be almost insoluble. If a book dealer is under-
capitalized, as is frequently the case, he cannot afford to wait
several months for payment. He therefore prefers not to accept
export orders. To stay in business, he needs a rapid turnover and
quick returns, and these are not a feature of the export trade in
Latin American books.

Dr. Benson makes all these points explicitly in "LACAP Report
No. 2." She says one publisher in Buenos Aires preferred not to
cash checks for small orders because of the expense involved, and
she adds:

> . . . The few merchants or publishers who were agreeable to handling
> small orders invariably asked that payments for shipments be deferred
> until a check could be written for a sizeable amount because of the
> cost of banking small checks. It was generally made very clear, however,
> that most publishers here and elsewhere will not bother with small
> shipments out of the country.

So many problems of such complexity might well daunt the
most stout-hearted, but they are only part of the picture. Writing
of Latin American book catalogs in volume 7 of the *Handbook of
Latin American Studies,* Mrs. Cannon puts the situation in the
right perspective:

> . . . A technical analysis of this type which surveys an unfavorable
> situation and baldly states its findings is far too likely to leave an un-
> sympathetic impression of books considered merely as statistical data,
> and Latin America as a place in which results are meagre (*sic*) and
> disappointing. . . . No field appears richer in interest and significance,
> and no problem in library acquisitions is more challenging than that
> of making available to readers in this country the American experience
> of life as Latin America looks at that experience.

As the problems were discussed at the first four Seminars, they
became a well defined area for attack. Because they varied in kind
and intensity from country to country, a flexible approach capable
of indefinite adaptation was needed, and it was found in LACAP.
Before dealing with the actual launching of LACAP, however,

something must be said about activities in three other areas which contributed to the definition of the problems and the search for a solution. These were the work done by UNESCO and other bodies to improve bibliography relating to Latin America, the extension of the Farmington Plan to Latin America, and, last but not least, the programs of the Organization of American States which led to the holding of the Seminars.

CHAPTER IV

Efforts to Improve Bibliography[1]

The efforts to improve bibliography and the book trade in Latin America are part of a much broader effort to promote free cultural exchange in the Americas, in which government agencies and international institutions, learned societies and individual scholars have all participated.

The United States Government has participated from the beginning in the Inter-American Conferences and the Organization of American States, and cultural exchange programs have been organized by the Department of State for many years. In the 1920's, the American Library Association's Committee on Library Cooperation with Other Countries appointed a Subcommittee on Latin America, renamed the Committee on Library Cooperation with Latin America in 1931, which encouraged bibliographical activities, including a project for a union list of Latin American books. The ALA continues to promote bibliographical activities through its International Relations Committee at the present time.

The 1930's saw the establishment of the Inter-American Bibliographical and Library Association, with the encouragement of the Pan American Union, and of the Hispanic Foundation of the Library of Congress, on the initiative of Archer M. Huntington, founder of the Hispanic Society of America. The *Handbook of Latin American Studies,* which was taken over by the Hispanic Foundation in 1944, first saw the light in 1935. It was the outcome

of a conference organized by the Social Science Research Council
and of the efforts of the Advisory Committee on Latin American
Studies of the American Council of Learned Societies, which
financed the original publication. Under its first great editor,
Lewis Hanke, historian and bibliographer, then of Harvard University, such distinguished scholars as C. K. Jones, compiler
of the *Bibliography of Bibliographies of Latin America,* Sturgis E.
Leavitt, Professor of Spanish at the University of North Carolina
and specialist in Latin American periodicals, J. Fred Rippy, historian, of the University of Chicago, and many others cooperated
to produce a bibliographical monument. The articles contributed
to the early volumes of the *Handbook* are full not only of bibliographical information but of the joy and excitement of creative
scholarship.

In the 1940's, the Hispanic Foundation embarked on its Latin
American Series, which includes the guides to the law and legal
literature and to the official publications of the other American
republics, Gilbert Chase's *Guide to the Music of Latin America*
and the Jones bibliography already mentioned. The Series is being continued for a guide to the law and legal literature of Brazil
is being compiled by Mrs. Helen Clagett, of the Law Library,
Library of Congress.[2]

UNESCO's bibliographical work is worldwide, but some of its
activities have been aimed specifically at improving bibliography
in Latin America. The UNESCO Division of Libraries, Documentation and Archives is continuing to support these activities
but it is now placing special emphasis on the training of high-
level librarians in planning techniques, with a view to ensuring
that library planning, including bibliographical work, is inte-
grated with the national economic and social development plans.

The International Advisory Committee on Bibliography—now
renamed the International Advisory Committee on Bibliography,
Documentation and Terminology—was established as the result
of the Conference on the Improvement of Bibliographical
Services, convened by UNESCO in 1950. Part of the Committee's
task is to promote the work of national bibliographical groups,
and by 1960 there were fifteen such groups in Latin American
countries. The Cuban bibliographical group under Fermín Peraza
Sarausa—the Agrupación Bibliográfica José Toribio Medina—has

been particularly active. It undertook the compilation of the *Bibliografía de Centro América y del Caribe* in accordance with a recommendation of the Pilot Seminar on Bibliography in Central America and the Caribbean, organized by UNESCO in Havana, Cuba, in 1955. This bibliography had begun to appear when, in 1960, the Regional Seminar on Bibliography, Documentation and Terminology, held in Mexico City, also under the auspices of UNESCO, decided that it should be expanded into the *Bibliografía de América Latina*. This vast undertaking, which would be an indigenous counterpart of the *Handbook for Latin American Studies,* has so far failed to materialize. In the meantime, UNESCO has assisted in the publication of less far-reaching bibliographies, such as the *Anuario Bibliográfico Colombiano, 1951-1956,* compiled by the Instituto Caro y Cuervo, and a union list of foreign scientific publications in Costa Rica. The list of reference works relating to Latin America, recommended by the Second Seminar on Bibliography, organized by UNESCO in Panama City in 1958, was published, with UNESCO assistance, in 1965. This is Abel Rodolfo Geoghegan's *Obras de referencia de América Latina,* a very handy and useful compilation. UNESCO also publishes some bibliographical information on a regular basis in two periodicals, the *Unesco Bulletin for Libraries,* and *Bibliography, Documentation and Terminology,* the organ of the new International Advisory Committee mentioned earlier, and in its reports on bibliographical services throughout the world.

Mrs. Shepard has given a thorough account of the broad effort to promote cultural exchange in the Americas in two articles, "The Contribution of the Organization of American States to the Exchange of Publications in the Americas," published in the *Library Quarterly* for January, 1958, and "Bibliographic Activities of the Organization of American States," which appeared in the *American Library Association Bulletin* for July-August, 1961. Only some of the salient points need be mentioned here.

Free cultural exchange has been one of the basic tenets of the American States ever since the First International Conference of American States in 1890. It is reaffirmed in the Charter of Bogotá and in the Declaration on Cultural Cooperation, adopted by the OAS in 1948 and 1954 respectively. Among other things, the

Charter of Bogotá provided for the establishment of the Inter-
American Cultural Council, which at its first meeting, held in
Mexico City in 1951, laid down a program for the encouragement
of libraries and bibliography. The activities carried on by the
Pan American Union under the Inter-American Library and
Bibliographic Development Program, which was organized to give
effect to the Council's decision, have also been described by Mrs.
Shepard, in another excellent article, published in *Libri* in 1962.[3]
The Program aims, *inter alia,* at promoting improved book trade
methods, increased bibliographic coverage, and extended library
services. The Pan American Union has acted in cooperation with
other organizations—such as the Inter-American Bibliographical
and Library Association and UNESCO—through its own projects,
and through SALALM.

UNESCO is not a sponsor of SALALM but it has been represented at SALALM meetings. In the paper which he submitted to
the first Seminar, Carlos Victor Penna, now Chief of the
UNESCO Division of Libraries, Documentation and Archives but
then representing the UNESCO Regional Office in the Western
Hemisphere, said:

> . . . The lack of authoritative national bibliographies compels Amer-
> ican librarians to make use of bibliographies which are not edited in
> Latin America, such as the *Handbook of Latin American Studies* or the
> monthly OAS accessions list.

In another paper submitted to the same Seminar, Robert Kingery,
Chief of the Preparation Division of the New York Public Library,
said that, although theoretically there were bibliographies for
nine of the Latin American countries, the New York Public
Library relied on the two above-mentioned publications and the
Revista Inter-Americana de Bibliografía, supplemented by the
UNESCO reports on bibliographical services throughout the
world.

There are, therefore, some grounds for stating that in 1956
virtually the only sources of bibliographical information readily
accessible to American librarians, apart from dealers' lists, were
the publications already mentioned.

This view is contested, however, by Nathan A. Haverstock, then
editor of the *Handbook of Latin American Studies,* in a paper

which he submitted to the fifth Seminar, in 1960. He says in this paper, "The charge that Latin America is backward bibliographically has been repeated so often that North Americans have come to believe it," and he suggests that two separate problems—how to learn about a book's existence, and how to acquire a copy—had become confused. Haverstock's view of Latin American bibliography is described as "unusually affirmative" by Father Brendan Connolly, S. J., in his "Bibliography of Bibliographies of the First Ten Seminars," prepared in 1965 for submission to the tenth Seminar, but it is supported by solid evidence. Even twenty years earlier, when the state of bibliography can hardly have been better than it was in 1960, Murray M. Wise, then Latin American consultant to the Hispanic Foundation, Library of Congress, could cite a respectable number of special sources and national bibliographies in the review of bibliographical activity during the past five years which he prepared for the 1939 *Handbook*. He does say, however, that the best source of information is newspapers and magazines or publications series in the form of pamphlets or monographs, rather than special studies in book form. In any event, Haverstock's view is based on positive evidence, obtained by circularizing editors and publishers, and he lists forty bibliographies in his paper. He also suggests that SALALM should focus on "modest attainable goals," including surveys of existing bibliographical tools and collaboration with Latin American bibliographers. SALALM has followed both those paths.

Realizing that bibliographic access was the key to success in the acquisition of library materials, SALALM has always paid special attention to bibliography. It has promoted the compilation of national and special bibliographies, with the accent on current bibliography, and the preparation of bibliographical tools, such as directories, indexes, guides, and book lists. It has also assisted other organizations in bibliographical work. One example is its cooperation with the Caribbean Economic Development Corporation in the future establishment of a regional bibliographic center for the Caribbean. The most recent developments are described in Mrs. Shepard's Progress Report to the twelfth Seminar. After a conference in March, 1967, further planning has been entrusted to an *Ad Hoc* Subcommittee on a Pilot Bibliographic Center for the Caribbean. If present plans are put into effect, the

future center will issue *Current Caribbean Bibliography* on a
current, regular basis.

One of the virtues of SALALM is the flexibility of its approach,
and this is nowhere better shown than in its attack on the problems of bibliography. It has no funds with which to finance publications, and it does not therefore usually engage in compilation
on its own account. There is, however, one exception to this rule.
The *Index to Latin American Periodicals* (ILAP) was undertaken by a committee of SALALM, which selected about two
hundred periodicals to be indexed in the fields of the humanities
and the social sciences and brought the project to a point where
direct negotiations were required between the sponsors—the New
York Public Library and the Pan American Union. The first
volume, published by G. K. Hall and Co., appeared in 1962.
Publication has now been taken over by the Scarecrow Press. The
fifth volume appeared in quarterly issues during 1965 and the
cumulative issue for 1965 (volume 5, number 4) was ready for
distribution when the twelfth Seminar met, in June 1967. G. K.
Hall also published the *Index to Latin American Periodical
Literature 1929-1960,* based on selections from a wider field made
by the Pan American Union. A supplement 1961-1965 to the
original eight-volume work has been prepared and it is expected
that reproduction will begin shortly. There is no overlapping
between the supplement and ILAP. The Pan American Union's
quarterly newsletter, *Inter-American Library Relations,* includes
a selected bibliography which contains items of interest to the
librarians of Latin American collections in the United States.

SALALM has achieved results, in large measure, by encouraging bibliographic work among SALALM participants. It has thus
made a substantial contribution to the amount of bibliographical
information available. In the bibliographical paper already mentioned, Father Connolly lists sixty-two items, to which must be
added that compilation itself and the bibliographies submitted to
subsequent Seminars. By mid-1966, SALALM had sixty-six bibliographies to its credit. Fifteen of the twenty-one papers submitted
to the sixth Seminar deal wholly or partly with bibliographical
matters.

In the report "Bibliographic Achievements of the Seminars:
Some Problems and Possible Solutions," submitted to the tenth

Seminar, Dr. Irene Zimmerman, Latin American Specialist of the University of Florida Libraries and Chairman of the SALALM Committee on Bibliography, is very careful not to claim for SALALM any credit to which it is not entitled. Nevertheless, she says that its recommendations may have helped to obtain financing for the indexing of the *Handbook of Latin American Studies,* and she lists forty-five "bibliographies partially attributable to SALALM" in the appendix to her report. Many others, in which SALALM had no part, are mentioned in the report itself.

In the field of current bibliography, Carl W. Deal, Latin American Librarian of the University of Illinois Library and Chairman of the SALALM Committee on Reporting Bibliographic Activities from 1964 to 1966, lists work in progress and projects recently completed in his reports to the tenth and eleventh Seminars. These are selective lists, but they present in a succinct and well ordered form an over-all review of the bibliographical information freshly available. William R. Woods, Latin American Bibliographer of the University of California, Los Angeles, who has replaced Deal as Chairman of this Committee, presented a third report of the same kind to the twelfth Seminar. The compilation of a list of unpublished bibliographies was under consideration at the time of the eleventh Seminar (1966).

Among the efforts which have been particularly welcomed by American librarians are *Libros en Venta* and *Fichero Bibliográfico Hispanoamericano,* which were produced by the R. R. Bowker Company in response to a need expressed by SALALM. Daniel Melcher, Managing Director of the R. R. Bowker Company, was a participant in the early Seminars, and he was impressed by the dearth of current bibliographies relating to Latin America. After financing the publication of *México Bibliográfico 1957-1960,* by Josefina Berroa, the R. R. Bowker Company began to publish *Fichero* in 1961, first as a quarterly and then as a monthly publication. It was followed by *Libros en Venta* in April, 1964. The supplement to *Libros en Venta,* which was announced for 1967, is now expected in the Spring of 1968.

The LACAP lists and catalogs also are a contribution to bibliography, and are mentioned as such by Dr. Zimmerman in the report already mentioned. The lists, *New Latin American Books,* appear monthly and contain all the titles received by LACAP

participants. They are, therefore, the most up-to-date record of
current Latin American publications. They are supplemented by
the LACAP catalog, *Latin America,* which appears at roughly
quarterly intervals and lists not only current but retrospective
materials. Special lists, such as *Books from the Caribbean* in 1963,
are published from time to time. All titles are listed by country
of origin. Although there is no attempt to give full bibliographic
citations, these lists are a useful record of current book production.

Besides many partial bibliographies, subject and national, relating to Latin America which are now appearing, there is a
whole series of bibliographical tools which did not exist ten years
ago. A selected list of book dealers in the Americas was published
thirty years ago in the third volume of the *Handbook of Latin
American Studies,* but it is very short. The Pan American Union's
Directorio de casas editoriales en América latina, the sixth edition
of which was published in 1958, therefore filled a felt want. More
recent information is available in *La empresa del libro en América
latina. Editores y libreros,* distributed by the Argentine office of
the R. R. Bowker Company. The Pan American Union's *Guía de
bibliotecas de la América Latina* is another useful publication.
Among the many other useful compilations mentioned by Mrs.
Shepard in her Progress Reports to XI and XII SALALM, the
following may be mentioned as examples. There are the begin-
nings of a Latin American book review digest in the *Guía a las
reseñas de libros de y sobre Hispanoamérica,* compiled by Antonio
Matos as a by-product of the "Current Bibliography" section of
Caribbean Studies. In 1966, a list of *Selection Aids on Latin
America for Primary and Secondary School Libraries* and a proposal for the compilation of a selected list of books for Latin
American university libraries were issued by the Pan American
Union as Cuadernos bibliotecológicos Nos. 32 and 38. A meeting
on the latter project was held, with a grant from the Council on
Library Resources, in June, 1966 and the Pan American Union
has assumed the responsibility for finding the $200,000 or so re-
quired for its compilation. According to the proposal, the list will
contain about 1,000 books and take about three years to compile.
Compilations relating to the Caribbean can be expected, both
from the Corporación de Desarrollo Económico del Caribe
(CODECA—the Caribbean Economic Development Corporation),

which has replaced the former Caribbean Commission and its successor, the Caribbean Organization, and also from the future bibliographic center for the Caribbean, for which Mrs. Shepard has fought so long and hard. In addition, universities with Latin American area studies programs are producing valuable publications, such as the two-volume *Guide to Latin American Studies,* published by the Latin American Center of the University of California, Los Angeles, under the editorship of Martin H. Sable. This lists about 4,000 titles but it does not mention any of the SALALM publications.

The Hispanic Foundation of the Library of Congress carries on bibliographic activities related to Latin America as a permanent part of its work, and it reports on them annually. The editing of the *Handbook of Latin American Studies* has already been mentioned. A cumulative index of volumes 1-28 is in preparation at the University of Florida. The author index has already been completed and will be published separately, probably during the Fall of 1967. The subject index is being compiled and will be published later in 1967 or in 1968. "Cuba: A Select List of Reference and Research Tools," a processed list designed primarily as a reference aid, and the Latin American section of the 1965 supplement to the American Universities Field Staff (AUFS) *Select Bibliography* were prepared by the Hispanic Foundation in 1965-1966. The latter contains 142 annotated entries.

A further expansion of the bibliographical work of the Hispanic Foundation was made possible by a grant from the Ford Foundation in January, 1964. The grant provides three-year support for the development of research tools and bibliographical aids for the promotion of Latin American studies in the United States. The Conference on Latin American History (CLAH), a professional body of U. S. historians of Latin America to which the Hispanic Foundation serves as secretariat, received a similar grant in January, 1965. As a result of the cooperation between the Hispanic Foundation and CLAH, two compilations by Dr. Howard F. Cline, Director of the Hispanic Foundation, have already appeared. One is the impressive collection of essays on the study and teaching of Latin American history, *Latin American History,* in two volumes, and the other is a directory, *Historians of Latin America in the United States, 1965.* A guide to the historical literature of Latin America, which will appear as a CLAH publication, is nearing completing under the editorship of Dr. Charles C. Griffin, Professor of History at Vassar College. Publication by the University of Texas Press is expected in the near future.

The first issue of the *Latin American Research Review* was published in the Fall of 1965 by the University of Texas Press. It was started as a cooperative venture by more than twenty U. S. libraries with major Latin American programs, but its Board voted to turn the publication over to the newly formed Latin American Studies Association as of June 30, 1967. It is now the official organ of the Association, which was formed in May, 1966, under the joint sponsorship of the Hispanic Foundation, the American Research Review Board, and the Joint Committee on Latin American Studies of the American Council of Learned Societies and the Social Science Research Council. It appears three times a year, and besides a topical review of the state of research and information on projects under way, it contains a considerable amount of bibliographical information.

Lastly, the new National Program for Acquisitions and Cataloging,[4] with the Latin American sector of which the Hispanic Foundation is deeply involved, can be expected to have far-reaching bibliographical implications.

Some idea of the growth in the number of bibliographies relating to Latin America since 1942 may be gained from a comparison of the number of entries in the second and third editions of Jones's *Bibliography of Latin American Bibliographies*. The second edition, published in 1942, contained 3,016 entries; the third, which has been revised by Arthur E. Gropp, Librarian of the Columbus Memorial Library, and is now ready for publication, contains over 7,000. Although the increase is due in part to the inclusion of new categories of material, it does reflect a substantial rise in the number of bibliographies available.

This account of bibliographical developments, although cursory, is sufficient to show that there has been a distinct improvement in bibliography relating to Latin America over the last ten years. There is still no over-all bibliography of Latin America published in Latin America, but there are many national and specialized bibliographies and a wide range of bibliographic tools. A comparison of the bibliographies mentioned by Kingery in 1956 with those now being published gives some idea of the progress made. Kingery mentions a handful of national bibliographies and three publications originating outside Latin America, which is meager compared with the impressive array of bibliographical publications now available.

CHAPTER V

Efforts of American Libraries to Solve Book Procurement Problems

Cooperative efforts to acquire foreign publications are no novelty in the United States. The history of the international exchange of publications is rich in examples of such efforts. It is not the intention here to give the history of these developments, but only to describe some of those which have had a substantial impact on present practice.

One program conducted by the Library of Congress—the Wartime Cooperative Acquisitions Project—is especially important because it prepared the ground for the Farmington Plan, determined the Plan's early procedures, and helped to establish the principle of cooperative acquisition as a means of ensuring worldwide coverage of foreign publications. Thus, although this project was concerned with Europe, the principles on which it was based had a wider application.

The Library of Congress

In their article on collecting in the national interest,[1] Barcus and Clapp say that the almost complete stoppage of procurement from Europe became a matter of serious concern to the United States Government during the two world wars. In 1941, an experimental division of library cooperation was established in the Library of Congress to deal with the problem. It worked out a program of cooperative measures, but the entry of the United

States into the Second World War prevented the plan's execution for the time being. The most important effort to meet the needs was the Cooperative Acquisitions Project for Wartime Publications—known as the Wartime Cooperative Acquisitions Project—which is described by Robert B. Downs in an article in the *Library Quarterly*[2] for July, 1949. It was organized to distribute the publications collected in Europe by the Library of Congress Mission. Although the Mission was mainly concerned with German publications, it also acquired materials in other European languages. The publications were distributed to the cooperating libraries through the Library of Congress. Between August, 1945, and October, 1947, twenty-six American librarians and document specialists were employed in Europe in purchasing the German publications of the war years and locating stocks of books and periodicals held for American libraries by German dealers. The materials were distributed to the participating libraries according to a system of priorities based on the Library of Congress classification. By 1948, 819,022 books and volumes of periodicals had been distributed to 115 participating libraries.

The project worked extremely well considering that it was new, and unprecedented in its scope. Certain principles emerge from the critical appraisal of the project by Julian P. Boyd, Librarian and Professor of History at Princeton and one of the framers of the Farmington Plan, in *College and Research Libraries*.[3] They may be summarized briefly as cooperative acquisition, bibliographical control, and division of responsibility. They have become so much a part of post-war thinking on acquisitions in the United States that few librarians would seriously question them now.

The weaknesses of the project, as well as its virtues, influenced the thinking of librarians. Boyd lists the weaknesses as follows: failure to exact a continuing commitment as a condition for high priority, lack of flexibility in the assignment of priorities so that a priority once assigned could not be changed, and too few classifications, which forced libraries to take more than they wanted. Libraries wanting books on dentistry, for instance, were obliged to accept the whole category of medicine. Boyd concludes:

> . . . Whatever may be said about the defects and inequalities of the project . . . it is nevertheless true that the Library of Congress is car-

rying to completion an enterprise that stands as a great landmark in the fast-growing movement towards greater cooperation among American research libraries.

Barcus and Clapp also commend the project in the classic article already mentioned, and they conclude that its most important result was to demonstrate what could be accomplished by cooperation.

The Farmington Plan

The principle of cooperative acquisition exemplified in the Farmington Plan took firm root. In 1962, the trend towards this type of acquisition was described as follows by Henry T. Drennan, then Public Library Specialist of the Office of Education's Library Services Branch and now Acting Chief of the Library Development and Planning Branch:

> In the twenty-four years since 1938 American libraries have dealt with insufficient financial resources, a great world war, a post-war period marked by continuing dislocations engendered by the conflict, population growth and shift, and a wrenching scientific-technological revolution. To meet these sharp problems libraries have adopted cooperation as one means of organization through which they can act effectively. If one can simplify starkly, the cooperative approach has been employed, mainly by academic libraries and to a lesser degree by public libraries, to bring first the tools that make books accessible and then later the books themselves.[4]

Writing in 1955, Dr. Downs, who was then Chairman of the Farmington Plan Committee, had struck a rather more sceptical note:

> . . . As a matter of fact, so thoroughly convinced are most librarians of the merits of joint effort that they are inclined to accept without critical examination almost anything with the label "cooperation" attached.[5]

Nevertheless, the actual experience of United States libraries with a nationally coordinated procurement effort is extremely brief, as Robert Vosper points out in The Farmington Plan Survey.[6] Boyd's assessment of the Wartime Cooperative Acquisitions Project is a clear statement of the general trend in the thinking on acquisition matters at that time (1947).

This trend finds more complete expression in the *Proposal for a Division of Responsibility among American Libraries in the Acquisition and Recording of Library Materials*,[7] which was drawn up by a committee composed of Keyes D. Metcalf (then Librarian of Harvard), Archibald MacLeish (then Librarian of Congress), and Julian Boyd. The committee and the proposal were taken over by the Association of Research Libraries in 1944, and the Farmington Plan, which grew out of the proposal, was finally launched in 1948, with Metcalf as its first Chairman.

A detailed history of the early years of the Farmington Plan has been given by Edwin E. Williams in the two *Farmington Plan Handbooks,* published in 1953 and 1961. It was first put into operation in Europe because United States libraries initially felt the greatest need for European publications and because the example had been set by the Wartime Cooperative Acquisitions Project. John Fall, Chief of Acquisitions of the New York Public Library, visited twelve Western European countries in 1948 and made arrangements with dealers to supply materials on a blanket order basis. The publications were distributed to the participating libraries through an office in the New York Public Library, which was thus involved in the Farmington Plan from the very early days. It was later to play an active role in launching LACAP.

During its first decade, the Farmington Plan firmly established the principles of planned procurement on a national basis, a division of subject responsibilities between participating libraries, and procurement through one local dealer, the Farmington Plan agent. Although Vosper says in the paper previously mentioned that the "Farmington Plan is not to be identified with any specific methods of allocation, acquisition, or distribution," it did in fact become largely identified with what he calls, in the same paper, "a subject-divisional pattern using assigned foreign dealers as selection agents." These procedures were subsequently modified as a result of the Vosper-Talmadge survey and the arrangements for acquisition from Latin America are considerably more flexible than the original procedures.

Remarking that "people who had been dissatisfied with the procedure tended to condemn the Farmington Plan in its entirety," Vosper goes on to say:

. . . The plain fact is that the Farmington Plan is not merely a means of acquisition or distribution. It is not necessarily tied to selection by assigned dealers. It is not irreconcilably (*sic*) bound up with an inflexible procurement procedure and distribution pattern. The Farmington Plan in fact expresses a broad concept, world-wide in scope.

The Question of a Traveling Agent

As has been shown, the peculiarities of the Latin American book trade presented unique difficulties to American libraries. By the mid-1950's there was a general feeling of dissatisfaction with the acquisition of library materials from Latin America. It was to discuss the problems and seek remedies that the Seminars on the Acquisition of Latin American Library Materials were organized.

Among the recommendations adopted by the first Seminar, in 1956, was the following:

> That interested libraries explore the possibilities and feasibility of maintaining on a cooperative basis one or more full-time acquisitions agents in Latin America.

Reporting on this recommendation at the second Seminar, Dr. Cline indicated that a two-year program of the kind envisaged would involve a relatively large financial outlay, and no financial support could be expected from other government agencies for the time being. He then put forward an alternative plan which was preferred by the Library of Congress at that time:

> . . . that of sending a member of its staff to a selected region of Latin America for a period of about 90 days to determine the nature and scope of publishing and the procurement possibility for U. S. Libraries.

The second Seminar accepted this alternative because of the lack of current information on the extent and nature of Latin American publishing. It was decided that the countries to be visited should be those about which acquisitions knowledge was generally the weakest.

It was thus that William H. Kurth, then of the Order Division, Library of Congress, set out from Washington on September 2, 1958, on the Cooperative Library Mission. This was a three-

month trip to Peru, Chile, Paraguay, Bolivia, Colombia, and
Venezuela on behalf of the Library of Congress and eleven other
participating libraries, all of which had agreed to share the cost.
Kurth was also to visit four other countries on behalf of the
Library of Congress alone.

In his "Report on the Cooperative Library Mission to Latin
America . . ."[8] Kurth gives a detailed account of his mission. It
was carefully prepared. Prior to his departure, he circulated a
questionnaire to the participating libraries requesting information on their existing acquisitions arrangements, and he outlined
the various factors and points that would warrant investigation.
The objectives of the mission were:

> (1) To secure information . . . on the production of research mate-
> rials . . .
> (2) To develop information bearing on the transmittal of research
> materials to libraries in the U. S., to secure data on bookstores, bibliog-
> raphies, . . . etc.
> (3) To prepare a series of recommendations . . . regarding the acqui-
> sition of research materials from Latin America.

Kurth visited all ten of the South American republics, and
from each he sent back field reports, which were distributed
through the Library of Congress. His voluminous report—over 300
pages—includes seventy-six field reports, a short report on book
production statistics, and a series of results and recommendations.
The information it contains about book production, publishers,
bookstores, and bibliographies helped to define the problems of
the Latin American book trade and to pave the way for an attack
upon them.

The first recommendation to the cooperating libraries relates
to the establishment of a procurement agent on a regular basis in
Latin America. Kurth says, "Personal representation for our
libraries is almost essential to provide publications on a regular
and systematic basis," and he adds that the need is specially acute
for government publications and periodicals, and much less so
for commercially published books. These considerations are followed by two alternative recommendations, put forward on his
personal responsibility, the first of which reads as follows:

That consideration be given to stationing a cooperative publications officer on a continuing basis in South and Central America; that the cost be met cooperatively and possibly also through foundation support.

The above recommendation is strengthened by the conclusion on the same point which is contained in Kurth's Preliminary Report. The emphasis here is slightly different from that of the main report, as the Preliminary Report was intended to support a paper by Dr. Cline on the possibility of extending the Farmington Plan to Latin America, but the conclusion holds good for both of Kurth's reports.

Kurth prefaces his conclusions in the Preliminary Report by a number of considerations, one of which reads as follows:

The maintenance of a cooperative acquisitions representative is necessary to assure continued systematic flow of research materials published by the government [and] non-governmental institutions, and periodical materials generally in the area of purchases and exchanges.

When Kurth reported on his mission to the fourth Seminar in June, 1959, Robert Kingery, as Rapporteur General, formulated his conclusion in the following words:

Mr. Kurth's conclusion is that maintenance of a Cooperative Agent stationed on the South American scene is preferred at this time to follow up the work of the mission. Such an agent must be a traveling contact whose presence, in addition to immediate material results, will be a manifestation of continuing interest on the part of North American libraries. This agent in his travels can stimulate improvement in exchanges, direct the flow of information back to the cooperating libraries, and aid in the program of the Farmington Plan.

Having considered Kurth's report, the Seminar adopted the following resolution:

That . . . one or more acquisition agents be established on a continuing basis on behalf of research libraries in the United States and that the area of operation be extended to all the Latin American countries.

The discussions at the fourth Seminar differed from those which had taken place at the first. In 1956 the participants in the first

Seminar had exchanged information and ideas with a view to possible future action, but by 1960 enough information had been gathered to indicate what form the action should take. There was a feeling that the Cooperative Library Mission had merely emphasized the problems involved. The cooperating libraries had received a great deal of information but their holdings had not been enriched. The stage was set for LACAP.

CHAPTER VI

The Specific Circumstances Leading to the Organization of LACAP

The specific circumstances leading to the organization of LACAP were the extension of the Farmington Plan to Latin America and the organization of the Seminars on the Acquisition of Latin American Library Materials.

The Extension of the Farmington Plan to Latin America

Robert Vosper says in *The Farmington Plan Survey* that Latin America is one of the cultural areas to which only "scant and scattered attention" was paid during the early years of the Farmington Plan. Eight European countries and Mexico were covered during 1948 and 1949, and the Plan went into effect for publications from Bolivia, Ecuador, and Peru in 1950. Duke University and the University of California accepted the assignment for those countries, and the publications were obtained through a dealer in Lima.

It was not until 1953 that there was a major break with the pattern of assignments by subject area. In that year, assignments were allocated for ninety-nine countries, including Mexico. This was the outcome of a recommendation made by the Committee on National Needs, which had been established by the ARL in May, 1951. In the *Farmington Plan Handbook,* 1953, Williams says that in October, 1951, the Committee "agreed that publications of some areas might have to be divided among libraries by country rather than by subject, and that the Farmington Plan ought to be éxtended to the Caribbean area." *Farmington Plan Letter No. 6* (November 18, 1952) announces that "Caribbean materials are being collected by the University of Florida as inclusively as possible," and it lists "critical area assignments." No Latin American country is included in the twenty-two regarded as "critical areas," but the principle that in those areas a single university should be responsible for collecting all the materials from one country was already established. When the time came, in 1959, to extend the Farmington Plan to Latin America as a whole, the entire continent was considered a "critical area," with the result that the principle of country assignments was applied.

The procedures of the Farmington Plan had given rise to some dissatisfaction owing largely to their inflexibility and to the fact that it had not been possible to set precise limits to the definition of a "foreign book and pamphlet that might reasonably be expected to interest a research worker in the United States," given in the 1953 *Farmington Plan Handbook*. In addition, there was a growing suspicion that libraries were not receiving all the publications they should be receiving under the Farmington Plan. The ARL decided in January, 1947, that the Farmington Plan Committee should, "in the light of its ten years of experience reexamine the purposes, scope and results of the Farmington Plan and report to ARL."[1]

As a result, Robert Vosper, and Robert Talmadge, then Associate Director of the University of Kansas Libraries, undertook the now famous Farmington Plan Survey, which has been well described by Vosper in his *The Farmington Plan Survey*, already mentioned. Two of their recommendations formed the basis of subsequent action in Latin America. The relevant parts of those recommendations are as follows:

> Certain operating patterns of the Farmington Plan, as they have developed in Western Europe, should be modified . . . looking toward a more flexible and decentralized procurement pattern. . . .
>
> The strengthened Farmington Plan Committee should give high priority to fostering and experimenting with flexible coordinated procurement efforts in other parts of the world, . . . ; in pursuing this task the Committee will need to develop effective relationships with the appropriate working committees in the several areas.[2]

The ARL Advisory Committee decided on March 19, 1959, that there should be specialized area committees with responsibility in certain areas, and it established a number of area resources subcommittees, one of which was to cover Latin America. The Committee specifically stated *"Farmington Plan* does not refer to a method of procurement but to a comprehensive plan of acquisition on a world-wide basis." Stanley West was subsequently appointed Chairman of the Latin American subcommittee. He has now been succeeded by Marion A. Milczewski, Director of Libraries of the University of Washington, Seattle.

Thus, by 1959, the Farmington Plan had become a more decentralized and flexible instrument for procurement than it had been during its early years. Although acquisitions were still to be made through Farmington Plan agents, the participating libraries were free to adopt their own procedures.

SALALM was naturally interested in the Farmington Plan as it applied to Latin America. Reporting to the fourth Seminar, the Permanent Secretary said that basic work on extending the Farmington Plan to South America had been done at the first Seminar (1956). Discussions had continued at the second Seminar and reached the resolution stage at the third, when Stanley West had been asked to convey to the ARL the "concern of the Seminar regarding the Farmington Plan coverage in Latin America as a whole." That was a strategic moment to act for the Vosper-Talmadge survey was under way, and fundamental decisions could be expected when the report was submitted.

Dr. Cline's report on the extension of the Farmington Plan to Latin America (Library of Congress, Hispanic Acquisitions Studies: No. 19) and Kurth's Preliminary Report were distributed to the fourth Seminar, which adopted the following resolution:

> That the Association of Research Libraries be informed of the Seminar's continuing interest in the extension of the Farmington Plan to Latin America and of the Seminar's wish to be of any possible assistance.

After considering the preliminary arrangements made by the Farmington Plan Subcommittee on Latin American Resources, the fifth Seminar (1960) felt that a review should be made before the final assignments were allocated, and it accordingly adopted a resolution to that effect.

A new trend was observable at the sixth Seminar, in 1961. It is formulated as follows in the *Final Report* of that Seminar:

> The concept of the Farmington Plan is changing from one of concern mainly for monographic publications from Latin American countries to one in which American libraries are feeling a responsibility to see that all important Latin American materials, including government publications, are acquired and housed within libraries of the United States.

This is in harmony with the general thinking on acquisitions upon which comment has already been made. From 1961 onwards increasing attention was paid to materials other than monographs. Textbooks were included in the Farmington Plan acquisitions from Latin America following recommendation by the seventh Seminar (1962). The question of periodicals and government serials was raised at the ninth Seminar (1964), and by the tenth, a "national acquisitions plan for Latin American materials . . . with special emphasis on such non-commercial materials as periodicals and government publications" was under consideration.

Cooperation between the Subcommittee on Latin American Resources and SALALM became so close that the Subcommittee's role was defined as follows in the *Final Report and Working Papers* of the tenth Seminar (1965):

> The . . . Subcommittee . . . serves as a liaison group between the Association of Research Libraries (ARL) and SALALM. Its primary responsibility is to convey information on the Seminars to the Chief Librarians who make up the ARL membership, and conversely to keep SALALM informed on ARL.

At the previous Seminar, Stanley West had pointed out that no other geographical area in the Farmington Plan had a working body comparable to SALALM, and that the Latin American operations had frequently served as a model for programs in other parts of the world.

It is scarcely surprising that the cooperation should be so satisfactory, since the Subcommittee is composed of some of the major personalities in SALALM, namely, Marion A. Milczewski, Chairman, Dr. Benson, William V. Jackson, of the University of Pittsburgh, Philip J. McNiff, now Chairman of the Farmington Plan Committee, Mrs. Shepard, and until recently, Stanley West, the former Chairman.

The Organization of the Seminars on the Acquisition of Latin American Library Materials

The Seminars were organized as part of the continuing effort of the OAS to improve the library and bibliographical situation in Latin America. The first Seminar was sponsored by the University of Florida Libraries and the Columbus Memorial Library of the Pan American Union, represented respectively by Stanley West and Mrs. Shepard. It was held at Chinsegut Hill, Brooksville, Florida and according to the introduction to the *Final Report and Papers,* it was "the latest link in the chain of cooperative efforts to resolve mutual acquisitions problems" and it "brought together representatives of government agencies, university, special and public libraries, Latin American bibliographers and scholars, the export-import book trade, international organizations and the U. S. Book Exchange."

The participants included Marietta Daniels (later Mrs. Shepard), the moving spirit and the future Permanent Secretary of SALALM; Stanley West; Rutherford B. Rogers, Chief of the Preparation Division of the New York Public Library, who was succeeded almost immediately by Robert E. Kingery; Dr. Benson, of the University of Texas; and Dominick Coppola, then Assistant Vice-President of Stechert-Hafner, representing Walter A. Hafner. The elements for a real attack on the problems of the Latin American book trade were being assembled.

The Seminar had a dual purpose, which is stated as follows in the *Final Report and Papers:*

1. To provide an opportunity for those persons chieflly concerned with the selection, acquisition and processing of library materials from Latin American nations and dependent territories of the Caribbean to meet together to discuss these activities as they especially pertain to major Latin American collections in the United States.

2. To assemble and disseminate information on the acquisition of materials from this area that could be of value to libraries throughout the United States.

Sixteen working papers were prepared by the participants, on five major topics. Two of these—"Selection of Materials and Bibliographic Sources" and "Book Materials—Purchase and Exchange" —are of importance for the present study. Dr. Benson, Robert Kingery and Dominick Coppola, who were to be closely associated in LACAP, all submitted papers and were active in the discussions. Edwin E. Williams submitted a paper on the Farmington Plan in Latin America, in which he stated, "Latin American publications have undeniably been neglected by those responsible for the development of the Farmington Plan," and "except for Mexico and the Caribbean, Latin America is not yet effectively covered." There was some discussion of the Farmington Plan coverage but no resolution was adopted on that subject.

Two of the resolutions adopted, in particular, were important for the future. One was the resolution regarding the possibility of maintaining one or more full-time acquisitions agents in Latin America, already mentioned, and the other, the recommendation that a second Seminar should be convened.

Thus, several of the factors from which LACAP was to spring were already present: three dynamic and determined personalities —Dr. Benson, Kingery, and Coppola—information on major problems as they pertained to the large Latin American collections in the United States, and a continuing framework for action and discussion.

The second Seminar convened at Austin, Texas, in June, 1957. In accordance with a recommendation made by Dr. Cline at the first Seminar, it had been decided that the work program should be organized geographically rather than functionally, i.e., by country rather than by problem. The second Seminar was therefore devoted to Mexican acquisitions, but the recommendations of the first Seminar were reviewed. William Kurth's trip for the Cooperative Library Mission was an outcome of this review.

One decision of far-reaching importance for the success of the Seminars was taken at Austin. It was resolved that "Miss Marietta Daniels be selected to serve as Permanent Secretary of the Seminar on the Acquisition of Latin American Library Materials." SALALM was thus assured of an essential motive force.

The problems discussed at the second Seminar in relation to Mexico were those which have become familiar in all discussions of Latin American acquisitions, namely, "out-of-print" books and private printing, and the organization—or disorganization—of the Latin American book trade. Francisco Porrúa of Porrúa Hermanos, the Farmington Plan agent for Mexico, estimated that perhaps 30 per cent of the Mexican book output was privately printed —a surprisingly low percentage compared with some of the other Latin American countries—and he suggested that in order to avoid missing the privately printed books, more librarians might place blanket orders. Kurth remarked that the Library of Congress had been satisfied with its Mexican blanket orders as a means of obtaining new books fairly promptly. This is the first mention in SALALM of the blanket order procedure which has aroused so much controversy and was to be employed so successfully in LACAP.

By the time the third Seminar convened at Berkeley, California, in July, 1958, the plans for the Cooperative Library Mission were fairly well advanced and were reviewed by Kurth for the benefit of the participants. In the discussion that followed, Mrs. Simonson's purchasing trip to Brazil, Colombia and Argentina for several United States libraries was mentioned, and the value of personal contacts was stressed. This is another principle which was to be successfully applied in LACAP.

Mrs. Dorothy B. Keller, Head of the Acquisitions Department, General Library, University of California, Berkeley, reported on her library's use of a blanket order procedure for acquisitions from four Latin American countries, but no details are given in the *Final Report and Papers* of the third Seminar. This procedure, which had received its widest application in the Farmington Plan, was already appearing as a possible solution of the acquisition problems encountered in Latin America by United States libraries.

The countries on the agenda of the third Seminar were Argentina and Chile. A well documented paper by Edwin E. Williams and Philip J. McNiff, entitled "The Acquisition of Library Materials from Argentina and Chile" and based on the answers to a questionnaire, discusses the familiar problems and their solutions as related to those two countries. Alberto Salas, of the Cámera Argentina del Libro, provided a "rapid panorama of the Argentine publishing industry." His paper brings out the difficulties and restrictions under which the industry was laboring, which he lists as shortage of paper, antiquated machinery, and problems with the copyright law. The appendices to these two papers contain a considerable amount of precise practical information.

After a general discussion and a pin-pointing of the problems at the first Seminar, SALALM had moved in the direction of a detailed study of those problems as they occurred in national settings. The trend was away from generalizations and towards accurate information, which was a prerequisite for any attack on the problems. Fernando Peñalosa's study of the Mexican book industry, an admirable doctoral dissertation which was later published in a modified form by the Scarecrow Press, and Kurth's report, "The Acquisition of Mexican Materials," both submitted to the second Seminar, set a pattern which was continued, with some variations, at subsequent Seminars.

Despite the decision to organize the work geographically rather than functionally—a decision which had been followed at the second and third Seminars—the fourth Seminar, held at the Library of Congress in June, 1959, was devoted to the question of library support for Latin American area studies. Kurth reported on the Cooperative Library Mission, which focused attention on the question of a cooperative acquisitions agent, and the Seminar adopted the resolution already quoted on the establishment of one or more acquisitions agents in Latin America.

The problems had been studied, and the solution was now clear, but the means of achieving it had not yet been defined. Only in informal talks outside the conference room was the real solution to take shape. There were some among the participants who felt it was not enough to adopt resolutions on acquisitions; something must be done. One of these was Kingery, another was Coppola. Between them, something *was* done.

CHAPTER VII

The Launching of LACAP

"LACAP was organized in 1960 . . . as a result of the deliberations and recommendations of the Seminars on the Acquisition of Latin American Library Materials," says the LACAP publicity folder. According to Mrs. Shepard, "LACAP is more or less in the same relationship to SALALM as the full grown son is to the father who spawned him." It is—to quote the folder again—"a cooperative enterprise that provides its participants with a steady flow of the printed materials currently published in all the countries of Latin America," and to achieve this purpose, it employs a blanket order procedure and a traveling agent.

In February, 1960, Robert Kingery wrote in *Stechert-Hafner Book News:*

> The University of Texas, the New York Public Library, and Stechert-Hafner are launching a Latin American Cooperative Acquisitions Project (LACAP) . . . The project is the result of more than four years of preliminary discussions and six months of intensive planning.

The preliminary discussions took place at the first four Seminars. Kingery describes how LACAP grew out of them:

> After the fourth Seminar on the Acquisition of Latin American Library Materials in Washington, a number of the participants gathered for a social evening. Inevitably, the talk centered around the concerns of the Seminars, and specifically that of establishing a traveling agent in Latin America.

The participants who gathered for a social evening were Kingery, Coppola, Karl Brown, formerly of the New York Public Library, and James W. Barry, then head of the Order Section, National Library of Medicine. They considered the possibilities and disadvantages of foundation grants and cooperative ventures before finally reaching the following conclusion:

. . . The final sense of the meeting was that a traveling agent or agents put in Latin America by private enterprise encouraged by the profit motive offered a possible, permanent solution to the effective acquisition of Latin American library materials.

Kingery goes on to describe how Stechert-Hafner became involved with the project:

Since Dominick Coppola, Assistant Vice-President of Stechert-Hafner, Inc., was present, it was both natural and perhaps inevitable that the others in the group should ask, "Why doesn't Stechert-Hafner do it?" That is the way LACAP started.

Kingery inquired about financing. On his return to New York, Coppola consulted his firm, particularly the President and Vice-President, Walter A. Hafner and the late Otto H. Hafner. As a result he obtained approval for conducting the project with the understanding it would break even financially within three years. Stechert-Hafner assumed full financial responsibility for the project and for any continuation of it, and it had the backing of the New York Public Library and the University of Texas. There was no formal agreement or sponsorship.

The next problem was the selection of the traveling agent. It is here that Dr. Benson comes upon the LACAP scene. One of the leading Latin Americanists of the United States, she was—and is—head of the Latin American Collection of the University of Texas Libraries. Her knowledge of Latin America was extensive, and she had already made buying trips to Mexico and other parts of Latin America for the University of Texas. Lastly, she was energetic, practical, and enterprising, and she knew the background, for she had been a participant in SALALM from the beginning. As Kingery says, she was a "natural."

In an unpublished report, Dr. Benson has described how she came to be involved. She was not present at the above-mentioned social evening at which LACAP was launched and was quite unaware of what was being planned when she returned to the University of Texas in June, 1959, after the fourth Seminar. She was, therefore, puzzled when she received a telephone call asking her to see Kingery in New York. She could not imagine why, as she was not on the organizing committee of the fifth Seminar, which was to take place at the New York Public Library in June, 1960, and she was "not at all disposed to go" for her desk was piled high with correspondence, and there was a big backlog of work that needed attention. However, Alexander Moffit, Librarian of the University of Texas, suggested that she "might just as well go see what it was all about," and so she did.

When she went to the New York Public Library, she was not told immediately why she had been asked to come. Kingery took her to a conference with the President and Vice-President of Stechert-Hafner and Coppola, at which the plans for LACAP were discussed and the need of a traveling representative pointed out. When she was asked whether she would take on the initial job of traveling representative, she turned the proposal down flat because of the amount of work awaiting her at the University of Texas, but by that evening she had agreed to take it under consideration; it was not until August 3, 1959, however, after many hesitations, that she finally accepted it.

During the discussion at Stechert-Hafner's, Kingery stressed that only a commercial bookseller could successfully undertake to supply Latin American books to United States libraries because only a commercial firm would have the technical know-how of handling and distribution, and it was agreed that whatever firm undertook the task would "have to keep one or more buyers in the field at all times to do the kind of job needed," Dr. Benson reports. As to the kind of person to do the job, "All agreed that it would have to be someone that knew Latin American books, knew the languages, and was willing to do a tremendous lot of work." And on this she comments, "just how much I never suspected until later."

By August 19, 1959, Stechert-Hafner was ready to proceed. While friends and colleagues worked on Dr. Benson to allay lingering doubts as to the wisdom of her decision, Walter Hafner made direct approaches by mail to possible participants explaining the plan. By January, 1960, LACAP was assured of the participation of the New York Public Library, the University of Texas, the Library of Congress, and the University of Kansas, although the Library of Congress had not yet officially placed its order. The blanket orders placed by these libraries did not cover all publications from all of the six countries—Ecuador, Chile, Peru, Bolivia,

Colombia, and Venezuela—which Dr. Benson was to visit. The Library of Congress did not wish to receive publications from Chile and Venezuela, for instance, and it excluded certain subject areas; the New York Public Library and the University of Kansas also excluded certain subject areas.

Financing

As has been seen, Stechert-Hafner assumed complete financial responsibility for the project, and libraries were asked to pay only for the books they received. Stechert-Hafner therefore paid all the expenses of promotion and organization and the cost of Dr. Benson's trips and salary, and advanced the funds for the purchase of books.

As little income could be expected from LACAP immediately, Stechert-Hafner decided to acquire extra copies of the LACAP titles for sale from stock and to use the LACAP trips to acquire out-of-print publications, sets, and other materials not covered by LACAP. These acquisitions were part of the firm's normal business in Latin America, where it had been operating for many years. LACAP became self-supporting within three years.

CHAPTER VIII

Spadework by Nettie Lee Benson and Dominick Coppola

January 15, 1960, had been set as a tentative date for starting LACAP. Dr. Benson arrived in New York on December 31, 1959, on six months' leave without pay from the University of Texas, and she spent the next ten days between the New York Public Library and Stechert-Hafner's familiarizing herself with the procedures, absorbing information, and seeking instructions.

The instructions were only very general. In the unpublished report mentioned in the last chapter, Dr. Benson describes them as follows:

> I was given very few instructions as to how I was to accomplish my mission. I was simply told to acquire all books that had been published in the last three years—1957-1958-1959—that I felt would be of interest to research libraries in the United States. Depending on the country, I was to try to get a given number of copies of each title I found and was to try to get bookmen or publishers to agree to ship the desired number of copies of new titles as they published them.

Dr. Benson was asked to buy several copies of 1958, 1959 and 1960 imprints (expressed as 1958+ hereafter) in each of the countries she visited. The number varied as the participating libraries did not all wish to receive publications from all the countries or in all the subject areas. It increased as new participants joined LACAP. Dr. Benson was also to look for out-of-print material, particularly sets, and to fill specific requests from other libraries, such as the Los Angeles Law Library. Just before her departure from Texas, she was authorized, on the initiative of Dr. Harry H. Ransom, then Vice-President of the University of Texas, to acquire up to $25,000 worth of books for the University. The New York Public Library set a similar ceiling on the purchases she was to make for its collections.

Armed with these instructions, a round-trip ticket New York-Santiago, Chile-New York, and great resourcefulness, Dr. Benson sallied forth on a trip which was to lay the firmest of firm foundations for LACAP.

She arrived in Quito, Ecuador, on January 16, 1960. The general problems she encountered there and in the other countries she visited have already been described and will be discussed here only in so far as they relate to specific countries or serve to indicate the magnitude of her task. The general plan was for her to visit Ecuador, Peru, Chile, and Bolivia, purchase what she could, and make arrangements with publishers and booksellers to supply new imprints as they appeared. On her return trip she was to check these arrangements to see how well they were working and, if there was time, go on to Colombia and Venezuela. There was not time for the last two countries, or even to cover the four others as thoroughly as Dr. Benson would have wished.

After she had been in the field about six weeks, attacking the task in her own way and reporting very fully and graphically to Stechert-Hafner, the need for consultation was felt. Coppola, therefore, flew down to Lima, Peru, where he met Dr. Benson on March 3, 1960. He spent one week conferring with her and accompanying her on visits to bookstores, *editorales,* etc., before leaving for Central America.

The technique used by Dr. Benson became a standard LACAP procedure, and it warrants some consideration here. On arriving in a new country, she compiled a list of books to be purchased from any bibliographical materials available, including publishers' lists, *anuarios bibliográficos* published by institutions and libraries, newspapers, talks with local residents, etc. She then made a round of the bookstores. Curious to see her technique, Coppola accompanied her on some of these visits in Lima. In a letter to Otto H. Hafner, he describes this technique as follows:

> . . . She introduces herself and the project to whoever is in charge. She is usually treated with a great deal of deference . . . They seem anxious to do business and [she] loses no time in presenting them with specific requests. First she asks to see the stock of 1958+ [imprints]. In each book she inserts a slip indicating the total number of copies which the publisher or dealer is to supply. For each book selected she writes out a slip to avoid duplication as she goes along . . . Then she checks the titles selected against . . . her bibliography and challenges the dealer to obtain them for her . . . Often they are quite successful. But as we move from store to store . . . 1958+ titles continually keep turning up.

Coppola continues:

> She is as thorough as one could hope to be. Her memory is phenomenal, her resources unlimited in her hunt for material recently published.

While they were both in Lima, Dr. Benson and Coppola discussed not only the problems of book procurement but the future of LACAP. The question of a permanent representative was examined and Lima considered as a site for a Stechert-Hafner office in Latin America, but nothing was decided on the spot. In the meantime, Coppola wrote to Walter A. Hafner: ". . . N[ettie] L[ee] B[enson] is definitely going to be available for another six months, beginning January 1961—the best possible thing that

could happen for the project in my estimation." In the same
letter he said:

> If the project LACAP is to be judged on how successful the coverage
> will be for commercially published 1958+ titles, assuredly it will be
> a successful venture. I really doubt that any other one organization,
> business or cultural, will be able to match the thoroughness of our
> acquisitions of 1958+ titles in the countries she [Dr. Benson] visits.

It is not possible to discuss all the trips made for LACAP, but
only to give some of the highlights from the reports sent to
Stechert-Hafner by Dr. Benson and Coppola.

Dr. Benson's Trip to South America, January-May, 1960
Ecuador

Dr. Benson not only visited all the bookstores in Quito, but she
made side trips to Ambato, Guayaquil, and Cuenca in search of
materials published in the provinces. The Universities of Guayaquil and Cuenca, she found, published some good material, but
it was not for sale and was therefore not obtainable except by
chance—if someone took an odd copy to a bookstore, for instance
—or by exchange. Even the publications of the Casa de la Cultura
Ecuatoriana, with branches in these three towns, were mostly not
for sale either. Nevertheless, she was able to obtain in Guayaquil
and Cuenca many works that were out of print in Quito. Dr.
Benson tried to talk the directors of the secretariats of the Universities into putting at least some of their publications on sale, but
without much success, although she had some hope of the University of Cuenca. She pointed out that if they did so, there would be
money for mailing publications when exchanges were arranged.
The lack of money for this purpose was constantly mentioned
wherever she went.

In Quito itself, the cooperation of the Casa de la Cultura Ecuatoriana in circularizing *editoriales* and printers has already been
described. The results were meager. Dr. Benson had some luck in
Quito, however. She came across a book dealer who did not have
a store and did no advertising but who had practically everything
printed in the entire country. He was not interested in selling to
bookstores and individuals because he wanted the material he
collected to go to libraries, where everyone would have access to

it. He agreed to sell to LACAP because the material was going to university libraries.

Although she had ample funds, Dr. Benson was not anxious to pay high prices for the materials she bought. She bargained, looked for alternative suppliers, and only paid a price she considered high when the material could be obtained in no other way. She was, therefore, somewhat taken aback to read in a Quito newspaper that she had come to acquire Ecuadorian materials *"a cualquier precio."* "The people with whom I have been dealing would certainly disagree with that statement," she comments.

Like most other Latin American countries, Ecuador has a depository law which is infrequently observed. According to the Librarian of the National Library of Ecuador, the reason for this is that the Ecuadorian depository law provides that either the author or the publisher shall make the deposit, and neither actually does so.

Discussing the familiar problem of finding "out-of-print" works which are not really out of print but held by the author, to whom the entire printing was delivered, Dr. Benson says:

> . . . The problem is to find who does have the material. . . . It is not necessarily out of print if you can find who got it. . . . This place at least surely is a demonstration of the need to get copies when they first appear on the market. It is practically then or never.

If LACAP has succeeded, it is partly because this necessity was understood from the outset.

Peru

Although the book business seemed to be booming in Lima, Dr. Benson found the assignment even harder to cover than in Ecuador. Many works by Peruvian authors were published abroad —in Spain, Chile, Mexico, or Argentina—and the works printed in Peru were often by authors from other countries, such as Cuba. As in Ecuador, very few imprints from the provinces were available in the capital. A Peruvian historian told Dr. Benson it was just as hard for him to get Peruvian books, living in Lima, as it was for her in the United States. He usually learned about them from scholarly journals published in the United States, and then had the same difficulties as she was experiencing.

Writing from Lima on March 20, 1960, Dr. Benson said that she was "very much dissatisfied," adding that the book business was "terribly disorganized," but the number of Peruvian titles obtained shows her efforts were not fruitless.

While Coppola was still in Lima, they had met a *corredor de libros* who went round picking up out-of-print material. Dr. Benson comments a little wearily:

> It seems to me that the name is not inappropriate for book buyers also, for one surely has to use a tremendous lot of legwork to find books in Latin America. It is a matter of seeking the books out in shops—large and small—on street stands, in warehouses, everywhere.

Chile

In Santiago, Dr. Benson met an official she would have liked to see in other Latin American countries, a *visitador de bibliotecas e imprentas,* who traveled constantly to see that books had been deposited as required by law. He had a list of every book printed and registered in the country. This was so extraordinary that Coppola thought it was too good to be true. Dr. Benson decided to ask the inspector to collect and despatch material for LACAP. As she did not wish to spend too much time visiting outlying areas, where she was told there was very little publishing, she devoted her energies to combing Santiago and placing continuing orders with a variety of bookstores for different types of material.

Bolivia

Dr. Benson reached La Paz at the beginning of May, 1960, after postponing her trip because of reports of street fighting there. She found the altitude and the number of stairs she had to climb a strain, but she struggled on. She reported that she had been busy trying to get as much material as possible and that "It is the same old situation except perhaps worse in that there are very, very few publishers. . . . Going from bookstore to bookstore literally hunting for the books published is both time consuming and wearing on one."

She had visited Cochabamba the week before, and had left just before a general strike was called. While she was there, she managed to find a bookseller who had a branch in La Paz and who promised to supply provincial imprints but she could make no arrangements for government and political publications. As an election was to be held on June 5 and a great deal of political material would be coming out, Dr. Benson suggested trying an agent in La Paz on an experimental basis. By this time her thoughts were beginning to turn homeward, and she flew back to Lima, which she left on May 31, 1960. She managed to write the LACAP report for the fifth Seminar before she took the plane from Lima, and she spent ten days in Ecuador, checking arrangements for continuing orders, before finally flying back to New York, where she made a last oral report to Stechert-Hafner.

Coppola's Trip to Central America, March-April, 1960

Coppola flew from Lima to Panama City on March 7, 1960, from coolness to 90° heat. In three days, he says, he acquired more education than books, but he managed to discover a few books as well. He found, however, that much of the publishing in Panama was done by the Ministry of Education, whose publications were not for sale. The librarian of the university provided him with a *Bibliografía Panameña 1955-1957,* which she had compiled, and she tried to track down some sets of periodicals but in vain. Coppola was equally unsuccessful in that direction.

San José, Costa Rica, was more encouraging than Panama City as far as available material was concerned. He found not only some new and recent (1958+ and 1950-1957) titles but a considerable amount of out-of-print material and sets, and he was encouraged to find two booksellers who seemed likely to supply more material. New books, however, were "few and far between because there simply was not much published." He says:

> . . . Of actual books independently published by commercial houses there is a distinct paucity. There aren't many Costa Rican writers, probably none by profession. A great deal of what is written here is done by people connected with the University and then their writings take the form of texts or monographs appearing in series.

As series could be obtained by exchange or were excluded from blanket orders because they *were* series, that type of publication was not wanted for LACAP. He managed, however, to secure enough copies of the *Anuario Bibliográfico Costarricense 1957* for distribution through LACAP, so the libraries would have something from which to select. Despite a discouraging start, luck was with him in Costa Rica, for when he was "walking briskly towards nowhere at all," he stumbled by accident on the only dealer of importance in San José, from whom he bought a number of complete sets of journals and about fifty out-of-print titles.

Going on to Managua, Nicaragua, he started looking for bookstores, but all except two were *papelerías*. He describes one day as being "a sort of chain reaction day." Starting with the librarian of the Biblioteca Nacional (who lived actually in the library), he received introductions from one person to another until he met "the only genuine bookseller probably in the entire country." Coppola describes him thus:

> [He] is probably in his seventies, calls himself a *"bibliográfico"* and comes from a well known family. He is a distant relative of Sandino, the rebel (Calvin Coolidge days), has a brother who is Archbishop and a son who had to flee to Honduras because he opposes the regime here. [He] lives in a row of houses which is far from attractive, and sells Coca-Cola on the side. But he has a collection of old Nicaraguan books which is unusual . . . . There are heaps and heaps of books in one huge room, stacked up and waiting to be placed on shelves when he finishes building a special room for them.

On the same day Coppola also met a dealer who sold current material, an energetic, ambitious man who was organizing a book fair and knew the current publishing scene.

The picture which emerged from this chain of contacts was not too hopeful, however:

> . . . I have been able to get a pretty clear picture of the grim book conditions here. They are similar to those in other Central American countries but more aggravated. Not even the government is much interested in publishing authors' new works (as it and the University were in Costa Rica). So the author has his book printed wherever he can, sometimes outside the country. Editions are usually not over 500 copies [many of which are given away thus killing possible sales]. Publishing, except for a few texts, is not a business. And even when books are placed on sale, they are much more expensive than [imported] books. So there also is no market for local authors and consequently bookstores display little interest in Nicaraguan publications.

He learned one interesting fact, however. There was to be a special edition of the *Pequeño Larousse Ilustrado* with all the references to Nicaragua corrected and expanded, an item which would be of interest to specialists.

The report on Honduras, written from Guatemala City, begins:

> I could really send this report on a postal card for about Tegucigalpa I have little to say except that the natural scenery was splendid and that business for us was practically non-existent.

Most of the "publishers and booksellers" turned out to be stationery stores and printers, but Coppola had an informative talk with the only important bookseller in the city, who told him that very little writing was done in Honduras—one or two novels a year and perhaps a volume of history or poetry. The "Biblioteca Nacional" had little to show.

Guatemala was "gratifying in some ways, frustrating in others." There was some current material to be had, the university press had an up-to-date catalog, and Coppola was able to obtain copies of the University's 1958+ imprints as a special favor. The frustration came in getting permits to visit government departments. Coppola describes the procedure thus:

> . . . I had to report first to the Ministerio in the Palacio Nacional. There I had an interview with some big wheel, who had his secretary type a letter of introduction for me, which he then . . . signed with a flourish. After that, the letter had to be stamped with a seal, in still another office.

Looking for a bookseller who would take on a continuing order, Coppola became almost discouraged. Most bookstores turned out to be something else or to have disappeared. He had a feeling of great relief, therefore, when he came across a successful bookseller who had already filled orders for Stechert-Hafner at another bookstore in the past. Unfortunately, the bookseller was leaving very shortly on a trip to Mexico. Unfortunately, also, much of his material was in storage and he did not quote prices, but he had some rare out-of-print material—some "one-sheet *decretos, boletines* and broadsides," Coppola says—and he was interested in supplying new books.

San Salvador was the last stop, and there the pattern was much the same—government printing and little bookselling activity—but Coppola found some out-of-print material and a bookseller to accept a continuing order.

Like Dr. Benson, Coppola was breaking new ground and finding the work often frustrating, with just a few rewarding moments. He could visit more countries in less time than Dr. Benson because there was less publishing being done in Central America than in the area she was surveying. He struck the key note of his trip in his letter from San José, Costa Rica, in which he says:

> . . . As I go along, I'm glad that we are doing Central America. Though purchases may be meager, we are at least establishing contacts in an area which has been absolutely sterile for us before. If we are going to count in the Latin American scene, we must at least have these contacts and be aware of the possibilities and limitations of these countries [as far as bookselling is concerned]

CHAPTER IX

A Pause to Take Stock

Dr. Benson's initial assignment for LACAP was from January to June, 1960, and she was to be available again for the first six months of 1961, but there was no one to cover the intervening period. After discussing the question with Dr. Benson during their conference in Lima in March, 1960, Coppola wrote to Walter A. Hafner:

> . . . [Dr. Benson] and I wonder if LACAP would suffer at all if July-December 1960 would be a period when we attempt to evaluate and absorb what will have been done in the first six months.

He pointed out that material would continue to arrive, both as a result of Dr. Benson's trip and on the continuing orders, and Argentina and Mexico could be developed by mail, adding:

. . . Then [Dr. Benson] could return to the field and bring all her
previous experience to bear on the next area at the same time checking up on some of the contacts already established.

By the time Dr. Benson reported to the fifth Seminar (mid-
June, 1960), it had been decided that there was to be a pause to
take stock. Before discussing the developments in LACAP as they
appeared at the end of 1960 and the work of consolidation during
the second half of the year, something must be said about the
fifth Seminar.

Introducing Dr. Benson's report, Coppola briefly sketched the
background of the project and Dr. Benson's and his own trips. He
announced that the material had been coming in over a period of
months and Peruvian and Ecuadorian material had already been
distributed. LACAP list No. 1 of Latin American books (June,
1960) had been published and was being distributed at the Seminar.

Dr. Benson summarized the problems that she had encountered
—difficulty in finding publishers and authors, unwillingness of
dealers to handle national works because of the small margin of
profit, refusal of university presses to sell their publications, sale
of publications in unexpected places such as barber shops, and
lack of money for mailing publications on an exchange basis. She
had thought it might be easier to find books in Chile than in
Ecuador, Peru and Bolivia, but such had not been the case. Other
familiar points came up during the discussion, such as the non-
enforcement of the depository laws and the problems of the exchange of publications.

One discussant expressed the fear that the operation of LACAP
might give Stechert-Hafner a monopoly of Latin American books.
Coppola replied that his firm did not wish to corner the market;
it was merely trying to get as much material as possible. Local
dealers were anxious to cooperate but a traveling agent who
would keep in constant contact with the book trade was a necessity if performance was to be maintained. Daniel Melcher said
that there was no need to worry about a monopoly, and Stechert-
Hafner would never get back the money they spent.
The Seminar adopted the following resolution:

That the entire matter of the cooperative maintenance of a traveling
agent for the acquisition of Latin American materials be delayed
until the sixth Seminar and that the thanks of the Seminar be extended to Stechert-Hafner for having taken the initial step in this
matter.

The Seminar also decided that, in view of the change in the situation created by the initiation of LACAP, it would be wise to
postpone the circulation of a questionnaire to libraries regarding
their willingness to support a traveling agent, a project which
had grown out of Kurth's report on the Cooperative Library
Mission.

The Farmington Plan Subcommittee on Latin American Resources had been established in 1959 and its members were all
associated in the Seminars. SALALM continued to be interested
in both LACAP and the Farmington Plan as means to facilitate
the acquisition of library materials from Latin America. They
were considered as two spearheads of an attack on a common
problem.

When the fifth Seminar closed on July 16,1960, Dr. Benson was
free to return to her piled-up desk in Texas and Coppola to deal
with the operational organization of LACAP. The interest expressed in the Project at the Seminar had been gratifying, but
a great deal of work lay ahead.

Although the arrival of books from the countries visited by Dr.
Benson had been a little slow at first, they had begun to come
in, with the first shipments from Ecuador reaching New York in
mid-February, 1960. The April, 1960, issue of *Stechert-Hafner
Book News* announced that by mid-April both the Central American material ordered by Coppola and the Peruvian and Chilean
materials discovered by Dr. Benson were arriving "in large lots."

If there was any part of her trip which Dr. Benson had found
more difficult than any other, it was the sector of government and
university publications. These were not only departmental reports
and statistical compilations but often literary and historical works
of value for research. The arrangements for obtaining these are
often complicated for they are only rarely for sale. This is one of
the problems which LACAP has not entirely solved, although
progress is being made. Some institutional publications have been
included in the LACAP receipts from the beginning but no spe-

cial effort was made to obtain them after Dr. Benson finished her third trip until 1965, when Baraya devoted a considerable amount of attention to them—with some success—during his trip to Venezuela. The Library of Congress office in Brazil is uncovering sources of bibliographical information which are greatly improving the possibilities of obtaining institutional publications in that area, but if the situation is better in Venezuela and Brazil, the same cannot be said about all the countries of Latin America. The problem remains, therefore, and efforts to grapple with it are often frustrating and always time-consuming. LACAP must persist in its efforts, however, if it wishes to supply everything of value that is published in Latin Amercia.

The original participants in LACAP were few in number— only five, counting Stechert-Hafner, as of January, 1960—but participation soon began to increase. Before the end of January, 1960, F. S. Mohrhardt, librarian of the National Agricultural Library, wrote to Stechert-Hafner saying that the U. S. Department of Agriculture had decided that it "might as well place an order for current publications." The University of Southern California and Cornell University joined in February, and several other libraries sent lists of *desiderata* with which Dr. Benson was asked to deal. Taking only the 1958-1960 imprints listed in the first LACAP catalog, *Latin America,* published in late 1960, 735 current titles had been distributed to LACAP participants and about 1,000 retrospective titles had been made available. The total for current imprints may be higher than 735, as undated imprints, some of which may have been current also, have been disregarded. LACAP was not self-supporting by the end of 1960, but by mid-1961 it was meeting its costs.

The 735 titles referred to above include works on such subjects as law, medicine, and agriculture, but the majority are in the fields of literature and literary criticism, with some philology, economics, etc. Some government and university publications, obtained mainly by Dr. Benson, are included also. Many of these titles might have been among the "lost books of Latin America" lamented by Vance Bourjaily if they had not been "ferreted out" for LACAP. As literary works, their value is uneven, but the aim was not to select only important works but to get as much as possible of everything which was currently being published and thus to provide an accurate picture of the literary output of Latin America. In some cases, Dr. Benson did not think very highly of the quality of the physical book or of the work itself but she pointed out that it was the type of material that was being published. It was valuable as an indication of the culture which produced it.

The value of political publications is another aspect of the same question. When Dr. Benson was in South America, during the first half of 1960, elections were pending in Bolivia and Ecuador, and all four countries she visited were producing political papers, pamphlets, and other ephemeral matter. Such material had to be sought out and it was a liability in her bags when she was crossing frontiers but she bought it because it was a reflection of what was going on in the country. Much of it can have little or no literary value, but it is not always the best authors who express the thought of a country more adequately. The important thing is to find out what the country is thinking and feeling; and who is to decide who are "the best authors?"

CHAPTER X

Nettie Lee Benson's Second and Third Trips: LACAP at the Sixth Seminar

Dr. Benson's Second Trip, January-July, 1961

In December, 1960, when arrangements were being made for Dr. Benson's second trip, one LACAP catalog containing about 1,600 titles had been circulated and another was in preparation. The catalogs contained out-of-print as well as current materials, but the total of about 3,000 titles for the year was a respectable figure for a new venture in a hitherto intractable area. Neither Dr. Benson nor Coppola was satisfied with it, however.

In 1961 Dr. Benson was to visit Colombia, Venezuela, Argentina, Paraguay, and Uruguay. Although only the New York Public Library had actually placed a blanket order for publications from these countries by December, 1960, she was asked to order seven copies of some titles, and nine or ten of others.

Dr. Benson ran into exasperating delays and formalities during the whole of this trip. She had to wait for a visa to Colombia, and when she got to Bogotá she was ill for a week. Later, she had to wait again for a visa, this time for Venezuela. She was held up by airline strikes on several occasions. In Caracas she was penned up in the hotel for one whole day while a population census was taken. Many of these difficulties, as on the previous trip, were due to political conditions in the area. Colombia was dealing with a recrudescence of *violencia* in some of its rural areas. Venezuela was going through one of its periodical political crises. Paraguay was suffering from the effects of a long dictatorship. Argentina was grappling with the problem of the *peronistas* and with economic difficulties. Only in Uruguay was the situation relatively normal, but normal in a continent where social and political unrest are endemic.

These difficulties caused her to make two unscheduled stops, one in Panama City on her way to Bogotá and another in Rio de Janeiro on her way to Asunción, Paraguay, and Montevideo. On both occasions, she took advantage of the stop to do some prospecting for LACAP, but she placed no orders.

In Colombia, Dr. Benson visited not only Bogotá but, in accordance with LACAP policy, a number of provincial centers also— Medellín, Cartagena, Cali, Popayán. She found there was comparatively little poetry and literature to be had in Colombia. The current books were mainly concerned with history and politics owing to the recent celebration of the 150th anniversary of the struggle for independence and the recrudescence of *violencia* in the rural areas already mentioned. The only other area where production was normal was law. According to local residents, the dearth of literary production was due in part to the people's preoccupation with the difficulties through which the country and the world were passing. They had no time for meditation and literary creation.

Remarking that her visit had been the signal for a number of articles in the local papers about the lack of publishing in Bogotá, Dr. Benson gives her own impressions in a report to Stechert-Hafner:

> I have been surprised by the fact that there is practically no publishing business in a place that considers itself the Athens of Latin America. . . . Today's paper had a long article lamenting the fact that Bogotá had no publishers at all.

Nevertheless, between January 9 and February 19, 1960, Dr. Benson was able to locate and have shipped some 138 titles which had appeared in 1959, 176 1960 imprints and 9 1961 imprints. Locating Colombian titles was particularly difficult, she reported, because they were "like needles in the haystack of imported titles," and the imprints from the provinces were not to be found in Bogotá. Even a Bogotá bookshop which had a branch in Cali did not carry the Cali imprints.

When Dr. Benson finally got to Caracas—having obtained a tourist visa for one month—she found the publishing situation very similar to that in Bogotá, the only important difference being that there were no second-hand bookshops in Caracas. She had difficulty in finding her way about in both Bogotá and Caracas because she could find no plans of the cities and many of the streets had no street markers.

Dr. Benson noted three firms in Caracas which had chains of bookstores, but they were mostly stocked with translations and foreign books in cheap editions. One of them, however, had a store devoted almost exclusively to national titles, a rarity in Latin America. Almost all the printing was done outside the country because of the high price of Venezuelan labor, but the entire printing was shipped back to Venezuela. As has already been pointed out, the imprint is far from being a good guide to the nationality of the author in Latin America. If the book is not actually published abroad, it may bear an imaginary imprint or no imprint at all.

After a busy few days in Asunción, Paraguay, Dr. Benson went on to Montevideo, which she reached on April 9, 1961, feeling as though she had been "put through a wringer," after struggling with the complications of air travel in a continent plagued by airline strikes. She found the task of rounding up about 300 1959-1961 titles and about 1,500 pre-1958 imprints difficult because book production in Uruguay was, as in many other Latin American countries, "practically all a maverick production," each author being his own editor and distributor. This form of book production was even encouraged by the government, which made long-term low-interest loans available to authors but not to publishers or printers. The "out-of-print" problem was particularly acute in Montevideo. Time after time, Dr. Benson was met with the answer "Out of print" when she asked for specific titles. Sometimes she knew that copies were available half a block away; sometimes a dozen or more copies were to be found in the bookstore itself. She says in one of her reports to Stechert-Hafner, "Now I can easily understand why all libraries trying to obtain books here have had so little success. I'm surprised we have done as well as we have."

After six weeks in Buenos Aires, where she arrived on May 7, 1961, Dr. Benson said it would need at least three months, and preferably four, to do the job "even fairly completely." Nevertheless, she had succeeded in locating 1,338 1959-1961 titles and about 1,500 pre-1959 titles in the space of six weeks. This was quite a feat, for the booksellers themselves often did not know where to find books they needed and asked Dr. Benson if she had seen them. For the fifteen or twenty publishers who were more or less organized, she found a hundred and fifty who were not, and these were the ones where Argentine authors had their works printed, in preference to the larger concerns. Dr. Benson says: "This fact makes book acquisition in Argentina difficult indeed."

In *Desarrollo de la industria editorial argentina*, which appeared in 1965, Eustasio Antonio García says the Cámera Argentina del Libro has 220 members. Deducting the firms which are not strictly publishers and adding about twenty small provincial firms, he gives 160 as the number of publishers, excluding those which are also booksellers. His figures bear out Dr. Benson's observations.

Coppola in Mexico, May, 1961

While Dr. Benson was struggling from Asunción to Buenos Aires, Coppola was visiting Mexico City to see the Stechert-Hafner agent and discover what was going on in the Mexican book trade. As he looked around, he noted the almost complete absence of imprints from the provinces among the books on sale. Thus, when he renewed his acquaintance with Felipe García Beraza, whom he had met at two of the Seminars, it was natural that this question should be among the points discussed. García Beraza, who was the Director of the Centro Mexicano de Escritores, thought that his organization might be able to help LACAP to obtain current Mexican imprints. Coppola suggested that he might try to get some of those from the provinces. García Beraza visited Cholula, Puebla, Orizaba, Córdoba, Jalapa, Veracruz, Coatepec and Tlacotalpan in the Fall of 1961, but complications arose with regard to the administration of the venture, and the arrangement had eventually to be dropped.

LACAP at the Sixth Seminar, July, 1961

Dr. Benson returned from her trip in time to attend the sixth Seminar, held at Carbondale, Illinois, from July 6-8, 1961, and she and Coppola both reported on LACAP. The difficulties described in Dr. Benson's report to the Seminar were discussed, and Coppola was asked about LACAP's plans for the future. He replied that LACAP intended to review the arrangements already made and to follow them up with check lists. This was to lead, *inter alia,* to Dr. Benson's third trip.

The sixth Seminar adopted no less than three resolutions relating to LACAP. The most important of them reads as follows:

> That SALALM express its gratitude to Mr. Dominick Coppola, Dr. Nettie Lee Benson, and Stechert-Hafner, Inc., for their pioneer work on the LACAP project, and that it give every assistance to LACAP in carrying out the third stage of its plan to expand its field trips to other countries, and to review previously established agreements with local sources of supply so as to acquire materials not received under these agreements.

Reviewing the work of LACAP, Coppola had told the Seminar it was planned to include Brazil and the Caribbean area in the program. Baraya's activities in the Caribbean resulted in a much increased flow of publications from that area, as the special catalog *Books from the Caribbean* (1963) shows. An attack was made on the problems of Brazilian acquisitions in 1963, but it was not until 1966-1967 that real progress was made.

In view of the fact that, although it had paid its cost for the first eighteen months, LACAP's financial future was uncertain, the Seminar adopted this resolution:

That United States libraries recognize their responsibility to support a realistic price structure for LACAP materials in order to assure the continuing success of the program.

The third resolution relating to LACAP provided that United States government agencies should be encouraged to cooperate with LACAP, "which seems to offer the best prospect for obtaining . . . the important books and documents relating to Latin America." The Library of Congress had supported the project from the outset. The National Agricultural Library had asked Dr. Benson to obtain one copy of all agricultural works, and it became a participant in August, 1963. The National Library of Medicine became a participant in January, 1963.

Coppola wrote to Dr. Benson congratulating her on the work she had done for LACAP, and he added:

> . . . It has been, obviously, a much more complicated and difficult task than anyone could imagine. Somehow we must manage to get across to the library world how really complex a task it is to obtain the current imprints of Latin America, at the same time, however, convincing them that it is a job that can be done as you have so well proven.

That it could be done was proved by the figures which Coppola gave the sixth Seminar (1961). In eighteen months, LACAP had been able to purchase 10,000 separate titles, 5,000 representative of the previous three years and 5,000 retrospective (pre-1959). Three catalogs had been published, and two more were in preparation.

Dr. Benson went back to Texas after the Seminar and Coppola to New York. For the next six or seven months, he was to spend time, among other things, in taking stock of the project and in improving the LACAP office routines. He had the idea of providing Dr. Benson with a new kind of check-list when she returned to the field. It was composed of slips, one for each book already received or in transit, and its purpose was to prevent duplicate purchases. The idea was sound and has since become part of the LACAP routine, but there was a certain amount of "debugging" to be done when it was first tried out, as Dr. Benson found.

In April, 1962, Coppola went to Bogotá to meet Guillermo Baraya Borda, who was to become the LACAP agent for Latin America. He also checked the performance of suppliers in Bogotá and in Caracas. His checking in both cities revealed that although LACAP was not getting perfect service, what it was getting was fairly satisfactory in the areas covered. He wrote to Dr. Benson:

> . . . The work you did in both countries was superb and . . . who-ever follows in your footsteps has a comparatively easy time of it. You have established a basis on which LACAP can develop steadily. With your initial work in the field and with regular follow-ups I do not think there is any other plan of acquiring books published in Latin America which can come anywhere near LACAP. We by no means have solved all the problems . . . [but] it is quite evident that we are covering the commercial output of Latin America more tho-roughly than it has ever been done before.

Dr. Benson's Third Trip, April-July, 1962

On this trip, Dr. Benson revisited the four countries she had covered in 1960—Peru, Chile, Bolivia and Ecuador. She had been asked to check the arrangements she had made on her first trip and to purchase any current titles which the dealers had failed to send. At the end of her trip, she carried out the same task in Panama City and Guatemala City, which had been visited by Coppola in 1960.

Dr. Benson found conditions, on the whole, much quieter in 1962 then on her previous trip. Everything was calm in Lima when she arrived there on April 11, 1962, even though a presi-dential election was due to take place on June 10. This had its inconvenient side for Dr. Benson, however. She explains why:

> I had hoped to go to Ayacucho, Trujillo, and other places in Peru but because of elections all my attempts to get transportation within the country [were] futile. Too many electioneering candidates—even all the poets, novelists, and dramatists were running for office.

She was "rather severely rocked" in Lima but otherwise in no danger. She never felt afraid on any of her trips, even though she was entirely on her own.

She felt commercial publishing was declining in Lima, but the

LACAP supplier was doing a fairly good job, so she went on to Santiago, Chile, at the end of April. After a trip to Temuco, she reported "It is fairly safe to say that practically everything is published here in Santiago." She had been disappointed to find that a press she had heard of in a suburb of Temuco produced almost nothing. She adds, "Of course, it is the few titles published elsewhere annually that will ultimately be the test of how effective LACAP is in supplying the output of these countries." She made what arrangements she could to cover the production of the outlying centers in Chile, particularly that of the university presses at Temuco, Valdivia, Concepción, Valparaíso, and Antofogasta. As the continuing orders were producing results, the picture of book procurement from Chile could be called encouraging.

In a report written from Cochabamba on May 27, 1962, Dr. Benson says, "I have been practically lost in the interior of Bolivia for the past week." As diplomatic relations had been broken off between Chile and Bolivia since April 16 as the result of a dispute over the waters of the Lauca river, there were no direct flights between Santiago and La Paz, so that Dr. Benson had to return to Lima in order to catch a plane to Bolivia. She left La Paz almost immediately for Cochabamba, and also visited Sucre. The LACAP supplier in Cochabamba was doing a thorough job and she found no new titles to buy in the Sucre and Santa Cruz areas.

The situation in Ecuador was less satisfactory. Owing to a misunderstanding over the payment of their account, the Casa de la Cultura Ecuatoriana, which had a continuing order for some of the LACAP materials from Ecuador, had ceased all shipments. This was the firm which had been so helpful on Dr. Benson's previous trip in circularizing all the publishing houses in Quito. She reported the difficulty immediately, and the matter was straightened out by the New York office. The firm started shipping new titles even before the difficulty had been cleared up. This case demonstrates clearly the value of personal contact. The misunderstanding would probably never have been dispelled by mail.

Another supplier had not kept track of what he was sending, with the result that Dr. Benson found some new titles which

ought to have been sent actually in his store. Ecuador has continued to be a problem area. Dr. Benson explains why:

> From what I have seen here periodic checks will have to be made in
> Ecuador. Furthermore it will take much more than just going to a
> store and asking about new titles or of looking at the latest catalogues.
> In every place by asking to be permitted to search in their warehouse
> stock I found more titles than were listed in the catalogue or of which
> they told me. The only answer is search.

"I never saw such a country for holidays," exclaims Dr. Benson
in a report from Guatemala. She arrived in Guatemala City on
June 27, 1962. June 28 was a holiday, so were July 3 and 4. She
was able to do the necessary checking in one of the bookstores
over the holidays and thus complete her task in Guatemala on
time only through the courtesy of the proprietor.

Dr. Benson arrived back in Austin on July 5, 1962, weary, but
comforted by the consciousness of a task well done. Although she
had felt the exhilaration of doing pioneer work and facing the
challenge of innumerable difficulties, she was anxious to get back
to her university work and her writing. She had written from
Santiago in May, 1962:

> . . . I do not regret what time I have put into the initiation of
> LACAP, for I think it is something that needs doing; but I think I
> have just about done my share . . .

No one could disagree with her. She had done a tremendous job.

CHAPTER XI

The Problem of the Traveling Agent is Solved

The question of a traveling agent was a complex problem
which had exercised the minds of the Seminar participants from
the outset. It was also a problem for the organizers of LACAP.
Stechert-Hafner obviously could not go on borrowing Dr. Benson

indefinitely, but a replacement was difficult to find. She herself had been aware of the problem and had discussed it with Coppola when they conferred in Lima in March, 1960. The need for some kind of follow-up became even clearer after her return to the United States, for although continuing orders had been placed, they produced only partial results, and the continuing flow of books was not so great as had been hoped. Even some of the books actually ordered by Dr. Benson on the spot failed to arrive.

When Dr. Benson's second trip was being planned, at the end of 1960, Coppola wrote to her:

> "The continuing service" from the countries you visited has been spotty . . .
> Certainly, . . . if LACAP continues to grow as we expect it will, the main problem will be finding the person who can follow up and continue the work which you have so ably performed.

At the end of April, 1961, when Dr. Benson was thinking of drafting her report for the sixth Seminar, she asked Coppola for an estimate of how good the service had been from the places she had visited in 1960. He replied:

> Needless to say, the picture of continuing service form Bolivia, Chile, Ecuador, and Peru, is a discouraging one. Although none of us expected too much, nevertheless you who made arrangements personally and went to such great lengths to achieve cooperation will be more than disappointed in the meager results.

Coppola was perhaps erring on the side of under-statement, for in her *Seven Year Report,* prepared for the seventh SALALM in 1962, the Permanent Secretary says several libraries had reported that their receipts of Latin American materials had increased tenfold as a result of LACAP.

By 1962, it was urgent to find a permanent agent, for Dr. Benson wanted to get back to her own work. Coppola felt hopeful of Guillermo Baraya Borda, a Colombian living in Bogotá. Although Coppola had originally felt Lima was the most suitable base of operations for the LACAP agent because of its central position, Bogotá was worth considering. By this time too he had become convinced that the permanent agent should be a Latin American who was familiar with the ways of the Latin American book trade. He also had to be hard-working, perspicacious, and able to withstand fatigue for he would be constantly traveling. When Coppola met Baraya for the first time, in April, 1962, he described the future LACAP agent[1] in a letter to Otto H. Hafner as "a personable chap, thirty-two years old and unmarried." A graduate in economics from the Universidad de los Andes, Baraya had gone into business and successfully managed a large supermarket for several years and then, tiring of this, he had started a book business of his own. He had become interested in rare books in his student days through his studies of the history of Cartagena, and he had acquired a sound knowledge of out-of-print materials, which he had sold to various dealers. That was how he had come to the notice of Stechert-Hafner, where his efficiency and businesslike approach had made an excellent impression.

In February, 1962, Coppola wrote to Baraya describing LACAP and asking him whether he had any suggestions for carrying on Dr. Benson's work. He received a thoughtful reply, the main points of which were: Stechert-Hafner needed a representative in Latin America who would be Latin American, well educated, familiar with books, and in close touch with the book trade. He suggested the firm might open an office in Latin America, the head of which would travel round to purchase material; from his own experience the acquisition of books was difficult in Latin American countries and close relations had to be maintained with the dealers. This was so much along the lines of Stechert-Hafner's own thinking that it was decided Coppola should go to Bogotá to discuss matters with Baraya.

Coppola arrived in Bogotá at the beginning of April, 1962, and he spent several days discussing LACAP with Baraya and getting to know him and his family. He found a young man of middle height with a reserved and studious appearance, good manners, and a realistic approach to business. His instinctive love of books and his social background—his father had been in the National Bank of Colombia and the family was well known and highly respected—together with considerable business acumen suited him for the job and enabled him to do it well. As his reserve melted and his imagination was fired with the possibilities of LACAP, it became clear he was the man for the job. The details took a little time to settle, but by April 24, 1962, formal agreement had been reached.

Baraya took up his duties in May, 1962, and by the end of June he had started on his first LACAP trip. In the meantime, he had spent a month in New York, familiarizing himself with the procedures of the Stechert-Hafner office and absorbing information, and he had accompanied Coppola to the seventh Seminar, held at Coral Gables, Florida, in June, 1962.

CHAPTER XII

Breakthrough in Latin American Acquisitions

The seventh Seminar (June, 1962) was a triumph for LACAP. Dr. Benson was unable to be present, as she was still in South America, but Coppola reported on LACAP and introduced Baraya. Coppola's report was felt to be of such importance that it was annexed to the report of the Seminar. It was also published in *Stechert-Hafner Book News* for September, 1962. The highlights of Coppola's oral report are given as follows in the *Final Report* of the seventh Seminar:

Mr. Dominick Coppola reviewed the history of LACAP, pointing out that it had grown out of the survey made by William Kurth, and from the recommendations of SALALM. It was blanket orders which made LACAP possible, and the project had made available some 15,000 titles in two-and-a-half years. Despite the fact that Nettie Lee Benson had spent a year in Latin America on behalf of LACAP, a subsequent trip by Mr. Coppola had demonstrated that standing orders with publishers and dealers were not being fulfilled. Stechert-Hafner has established an office in Bogotá, in the charge of Sr. Guillermo Baraya Borda, which will attempt to procure additional materials for LACAP.

In the discussion which followed, Francis H. Henshaw, Head of the Order Division, Library of Congress, and Dr. Felix Reichmann, Assistant Director of the Cornell University Libraries, "endorsed the work of LACAP, stating that the single invoices and the good coverage made comprehensive orders economical in the long run."

The Farmington Plan Subcommittee on Latin American Resources reported to the same Seminar through Stanley West, its Chairman, and the librarians of institutions which had accepted Farmington Plan assignments in Latin America. Syracuse University, which had the assignment for Argentina, Paraguay, and Uruguay, had checked its receipts against the titles in *Fichero* over a period of seventeen months and discovered 159 titles which it had not received. Most of the other Farmington Plan libraries felt that their coverage was not complete, particularly of periodicals and government documents. *Farmington Plan Letter No. 17* notes that the reports to the seventh Seminar indicated that "in nearly every country, the Latin American Cooperative Acquisitions Project . . . has succeeded in obtaining more material than the local agents engaged by the Farmington Plan libraries."

This was not unexpected, as West had reported to the fifty-seventh meeting of the Association of Research Libraries that book distribution in Latin America was not organized and that American libraries were probably receiving "only a small fraction of the book production of Latin America." The members of the Farmington Plan Subcommittee on Latin American Resources, who were all participants in the Seminars, were fully conversant with what they were to call in one of their later reports to the ARL "the vexing Latin American procurement problem." The libraries which had accepted Farmington Plan assignments for Latin America had been left free to make their own acquisitions arrangements, but the results were still disappointing.

After considering both the LACAP and the Farmington Plan reports, the Seminar adopted the following resolution:

> That Stechert-Hafner be commended for its support and maintenance of the Latin American Cooperative Acquisitions Project (LACAP), and that institutions, especially those with Farmington Plan commitments, be urged to avail themselves of this service in order to assure its continuance and extension into other kinds of publications, as well as commercial ones.

The ARL was kept informed of these developments. In his report to the sixty-first meeting of the ARL on behalf of the Subcommittee, West discussed acquisitions from Argentina, Brazil, and Mexico, and he welcomed the fact that other libraries besides those with primary responsibility for those countries were acquiring materials from them. After paying a tribute to the competence of the University of Illinois, which had the assignment for Brazil, he said:

> It is good news, however, that Vanderbilt University has assumed secondary Farmington Plan responsibility for Brazil, Chile and Colombia, and has issued blanket orders to the Stechert-Hafner's Latin American Cooperative Acquisitions Project for all publications which that firm can secure.

He noted that other universities had placed blanket orders for Mexican publications, for which the University of Texas had the Farmington Plan assignment. (Although the University of Texas is a participant in LACAP, its blanket order does not cover Mexico, where it has long-standing and satisfactory arrangements with Porrúa Hermanos). West concluded:

> The above, of course, does not mean that a copy of every major publication in Latin America is finding its way into a library in the United States; however, with the unprecedented interest in Latin America on the part of the Federal government, the foundations, and the universities themselves, and with the gradual assumption of responsibility for supplying Latin American books by book dealers in the United States and in Latin America, there is more cause to feel confident of a reasonable coverage of the publications of this continent than ever before.

As Coppola pointed out in his report to the seventh Seminar, the results of LACAP had been phenomenal, all the more so as the LACAP receipts did not include translations, textbooks, children's literature, unrevised reprints or government and society publications, which form the greater part of Latin American publishing. In actual fact, the receipts did include some government and society publications, but these were so few in number as to be negligible. The report gives 2,279 as the total number of

1961 imprints received from fourteen countries by mid-June, 1962, which was already a considerable advance on the receipts of 1960 imprints, but it was not the final figure. The final count of 1961 imprints as of April, 1967, was 3,258 titles, double the figure for 1960 imprints. The total number of imprints for each year of publication was to remain at roughly 3,000 from then on, with a peak of 5,309 for the 1964 imprints.

Coppola concluded his report by pointing out that LACAP had only just begun and, as time went on, it must turn its attention to the more difficult problems of government publictaions and periodicals. He adds, however:

> . . . Its continual objective, though, must be to keep acquiring current materials on the spot and to check the many arrangements made for continuing service from all countries, revising them as often as necessary.

He points out that it would be over-optimistic to expect all the promises of continuing service to be kept; that was why Stechert-Hafner had opened a Latin American office and engaged Baraya to operate throughout Latin America.

LACAP was approaching the end of its proving period in June, 1962, and was well on its way to becoming self-supporting. It was to continue on the same basic lines, but there were to be improvements in coverage owing to improved control by the New York office, supported by Baraya's checking trips. There were also to be improvements in the office routine, increased participation, which began to extend beyond the United States, and a sustained attack on the problem of government and society publications. Those concerned with LACAP have reason to be proud of its achievements, which are due in large measure to the vision and hard work of Dominick Coppola.

CHAPTER XIII

Putting the "Traveling" into "Traveling Agent"

When Baraya returned to Bogotá in June, 1962, he had a great deal of work ahead of him, since he had to familiarize himself with a vast territory stretching from Yucatan to Tierra del Fuego and to make the acquaintance of all the LACAP dealers. In the next two years he was to spend more time on the road than in his office and to visit all the countries in South America, Central America, and the Caribbean, some of them several times. It is impossible to describe all these trips in detail. All that can be done here is to trace the main itineraries and give some of the highlights.

The first country which Baraya visited, in July, 1962, was Argentina, and he went on from there to Uruguay, Paraguay, and Brazil, returning to Bogotá at the end of August. From March to July, 1962, Dr. Benson was revisiting Ecuador, Peru, Bolivia, and Chile, which she had covered on her first trip, in 1960, and taking in two of those visited by Coppola—Panama and Guatemala. By 1962, the character of the trips had changed. Although there was still some pioneering work to be done, particularly in Brazil, the principal aim of the 1962 trips was to check the performance of suppliers, ascertain why so many titles had not arrived, and take whatever action was needed to ensure future supplies.

The system of slips (the new kind of checklist mentioned earlier) had now been perfected, so that whoever was in the field had a complete record of all LACAP titles already received or in transit. Dr. Benson, or Baraya, as the case might be, was asked to seek out titles which were known but had not arrived and to discover unknown new titles. This became a standard LACAP procedure and is one of the major reasons for its success. Current imprints are tracked down before they can go out of print.

In Buenos Aires Baraya made the rounds of all the booksellers he could find. It was no easy task for many had changed their addresses, and he discovered, like Dr. Benson before him, that many of the streets had no street markers. He found the economic situation bad and many booksellers interested only in orders for a hundred copies or more. Nevertheless he discovered over two hundred 1960+ imprints and made new arrangements for LACAP books to be supplied both from Buenos Aires and from the provinces. In addition, he found a considerable amount of out-of-print material and showed himself to be well aware of values and prices.

He describes the situation in Montevideo as follows in one of his reports to Stechert-Hafner:

> Only very few titles I found in local bookstores in Montevedio. . . . After several investigations, because this job is something like secret service, I went to the Biblioteca Nacional of Montevideo in order to obtain some help. I found there above 80 new titles. But the problem was where to find them. . . . Some of the Uruguayan authors publish only 150 to 200 copies and they sell the books to friends.

Realizing he had no time to do the detective work required to find the authors or to buy the books, Baraya left the matter in the hands of a Uruguayan bookseller and went on to Paraguay. Coppola suggested that Baraya should write to the bookseller and ask him to check with the Biblioteca Nacional in order to keep track of new publications, which Baraya subsequently did.

Book production in Paraguay was so small that Baraya spent only a few days in Asunción before going on to Brazil, where he made formal arrangements with an old-established bookseller in Rio de Janeiro to provide Brazilian publications. The inclusion of Brazil in LACAP was announced in the September, 1962, issue of *Stechert-Hafner Book News*. This was the first step towards improving the flow of LACAP publications from that enormous country, but it was not until Dr. A. W. Bork, Director of the Latin American Institute of Southern Illinois University, visited the country in 1963 that Stechert-Hafner had the facts on which to base a better planned procurement effort. In the meantime, Baraya was turning his attention to Colombian publishing outside Bogotá, and visiting Tunja, Cartagena, Barranquilla, and

Santa Marta. In New York, Coppola was planning an investigation of the Caribbean.

There was almost no period during 1963 when someone was not traveling for LACAP. Baraya made three separate trips: to the Caribbean, Puerto Rico, and Venezuela; to Cali, Medellín and Popayán, inside Colombia; and to Uruguay and Argentina, for the second time, and to Chile. Coppola and the two heads of the firm visited Puerto Rico in September after going to Bogotá to see Baraya and inspect the Bogotá office; and Dr. Bork spent six weeks in Brazil. The eighth Seminar, held at Madison, Wisconsin, in July, 1963, was devoted to Brazil, and as the resolution on LACAP adopted by the Seminar relates mainly to LACAP activities there, the Seminar and Dr. Bork's trip will be dealt with separately.

Coppola had written to Baraya in November, 1962, discussing plans for the Caribbean trip and for Venezuela, Colombia, and Mexico. By this time, the regular LACAP order was for ten copies of current titles. Participation had increased and the Project was getting into its stride. Not all the problems were solved, but they were being defined and attacked, and the books were flowing in.

The Caribbean was *terra incognita* to Baraya, and it presented special difficulties. It consists of many scattered islands, some of which—such as Puerto Rico, Cuba, and the island shared by Haiti and the Dominican Republic—are large and some small— the Leeward and the Windward Islands and the Lesser Antilles, for instance. Guyana (formerly British Guiana), French Guiana and Surinam (formerly Dutch Guiana), on the coast of the South American continent, are also included in the area. Because of their colonial past, English, French or Dutch is spoken as well as Spanish as an official language, and there are a number of local languages, such as Papiamento. The whole area is under-developed, and political unrest is common. For these reasons, there was little likelihood of the Caribbean becoming a rich source of LACAP titles. On the other hand, anything that could be obtained from that area would be of interest because very few Caribbean imprints were reaching the United States outside the University of Florida. In any event, it was necessary to discover the actual situation.

Arriving in Kingston, Jamaica, on January 13, 1962, Baraya found some flourishing bookstores, but they were mainly stocked with English books. There was little publishing in Kingston itself, and none at all outside. Book hunting was not easy, since the bookstores—like the other stores—were open only a few hours a day. Haiti was more rewarding because of its greater cultural activity. There were ten bookstores in Port-au-Prince, one of which was most unusual. Baraya describes it thus:

> This [a bookshop selling works on the history of Haiti] is one of the most interesting bookshops I have ever seen. The owner . . . is the Director of the National Museum of Haiti. The bookstore is closed all day and visitors must call for an appointment. [There is] a good stock of out of print material on Haiti from 1800 . . . to date.

If business methods were slow in Jamaica, where no one worked more than five hours a day, they seem to have been even slower in Haiti, at least in the above instance.

Although Baraya had to interrupt his trip for a whole month in February, 1962, because of illness in his family, he managed to cover the Dominican Republic, Puerto Rico, Trinidad, British Guiana, Surinam, French Guiana, and some of Venezuela. In view of recent events, his comment on the Dominican Republic is of interest:

> . . . The literary and scientific production of the Republica Dominicana has been very poor, since this country has been managed by one family for the last thirty-five years. Nobody wrote a book without the censorship of the government.

As some concern had been expressed by the head of the Order Division, Library of Congress, regarding the acquisition of Venezuelan materials, Stechert-Hafner was anxious to improve the service from that area. Baraya therefore went on to Caracas at the end of his Caribbean trip. He was mainly concerned with the publications of non-profit institutions, which are responsible for a substantial amount of the publishing in Venezuela, but he managed to make some arrangements for the supply of current commercially printed publications also. The only town outside Caracas he was able to visit was Maracaibo, where he established personal contacts but found no books. His last stop was Curaçao, which he calls "a very little Dutch colony." Nevertheless, he found twenty-seven titles to order, which is a respectable number for a small place with only three bookstores.

After two months in Bogotá, Baraya started off again, in July, to visit three provincial Colombian towns, as already mentioned. At Cali, he visited the Universidad del Valle, a new institution run on American lines which is now a participant in LACAP, and at Medellín he paid his first visit to the Inter-American Library School, founded with the support of the Rockefeller Foundation and with the collaboration of the OAS for the training of Latin American librarians.

In November, 1963, Baraya returned to Uruguay, to check the performance of the dealers with whom he had placed continuing orders in 1962, and also to conclude arrangements for the purchase of a private collection. When the negotiations were successfully concluded, at the beginning of December, 1963, he went on to Buenos Aires. The firm which had received the LACAP order had sent nearly all the books expected of it. The standard of performance was beginning to improve. This was confirmed when Baraya visited Santiago, Chile, on his way back to Bogotá from Buenos Aires in December, 1963. There he found that the firm which had the LACAP order had done a thorough job, and he did not find any new material to send.

By the end of 1963 Baraya had familiarized himself with his territory and was making repeat visits to different countries. His work for LACAP had taken on a steady rhythm: he established contacts, gave a continuing order to the best suppliers of current titles (continuing orders for different types of material are often placed with several different dealers in the same country or city), checked the suppliers' performance, and ironed out any difficulties by personal visits. The procedure is not complicated, but it must be followed regularly and conscientiously. The knowledge that any falling-off in performance would be followed by a visit from Baraya and an inquiry on the spot made dealers realize that commitments must be respected; and as difficulties were ironed out by personal contact and the volume of their sales increased they saw it was in their own interest to be businesslike. The success of the method is reflected in the increased flow of books (for figures from 1960 to 1965, see appendix I).

There were two areas where the LACAP methods was put to a particularly severe test. One was Ecuador, which Baraya visited in the Spring of 1964, along with Peru and Bolivia, and the other was Central America, to which he made a trip in the Fall of the same year.

As Ecuador was one of the most difficult countries for LACAP, Coppola suggested that Baraya should place the emphasis on actual purchases of materials. He was able to make arrangements to cover the publications appearing both in Quito and the provinces—Cuenca, Ambato, Guayaquil, and Loja—and to confirm that LACAP was receiving good service on official publications. For a "difficult" country the results were respectable.

Baraya found that the LACAP arrangements for obtaining books from Peru and Bolivia were fairly satisfactory, although he was obliged to buy from a porter at an institution in Lima. Coppola wrote to Baraya on his return to Bogotá in March, 1964, "You should now have a pretty well-rounded picture of the South American book world since you have been to every one of the countries."

It would be tedious to give a detailed account of the trip which Baraya made to the other "difficult" area—Central America—in the Fall of 1964. Suffice it to say that he visited Costa Rica, Nicaragua, Guatemala, Honduras, El Salvador, and Panama from October to November, carrying out the regular routine of checking and purchasing. His trip is made memorable, however, by one report from Nicaragua, which is mentioned in *Stechert-Hafner Book News* for January 1965. No account of Baraya's peregrinations would be complete without it.

In Nicaragua, Baraya went to Bluefields to investigate printing there at the request of Stanley West. When he wished to return to Managua, all airplane flights were suspended because of the winter storms, so he and two friends decided to travel back by land. The rest is best told in his own words:

> We rented a boat to go from Bluefields to La Esperanza . . . going south along the Rio Escondido.
> We sailed at 4.30 a. m. from Bluefields. This was really an adventure.
> My hand bag with the books of Bluefields fell into the river but was

recovered. Some of the papers and five books were completely wet. Traveling across the jungle we reached La Esperanza six hours later still in the rain. At 2 p. m. we found accommodations in a local bus (small truck) with all kinds of packages, fruits, chickens and a small pig, and of course, twelve persons. What an experience! Then we spent eleven hours from La Esperanza to Managua because the road is indeed a very bad one.

We had no reservations at the hotels and a military convention was being staged, so it was necessary to spend the night doing everything except resting. Next day I went to Panama City.

Apart from the discomfort this trip was an adventure similar to the travels of Hernando de Soto, . . . but it was amusing and I enjoyed myself.

Although Baraya was not called upon to make such heroic efforts all the time, he spent nearly all the first half of 1965 traveling. In January, he visited six provincial centers in Colombia—Bucaramanga for the first time. In March he was off again, this time to Venezuela, where he pursued institutional publications with considerable tenacity and some success, besides tracking down commercial publications, in Caracas, Maracaibo, Cumaná, Barquisimeto, Mérida, Valencia, and Puerto Cabello. In May and June, he accompanied the Assistant Director of the Hispanic Foundation to Lima, Santiago, Buenos Aires and Montevideo, and helped him to survey those areas from the point of view of their suitability as locations for future Library of Congress field offices.

In 1967, Baraya spent some time in Peru and Ecuador, checking the existing arrangements, and then went on to Brazil, where he spent several months making preliminary arrangements for the opening of the new Stechert-Hafner office in Rio, pending the arrival of Coppola, who took the final decisions about staff, organization and procedures and appointed the Director. An account of these arrangements is given in the chapter on Brazil. Baraya stayed on for a while after the new Director was appointed to show him the ropes, and then returned to Bogotá in June. He now has responsibility for the Rio office as well as the one in Bogotá.

CHAPTER XIV

LACAP in Brazil

Dr. Bork's Trip, May-June, 1963

As has already been mentioned, Coppola told the sixth Seminar, in July, 1961, that it was planned to extend LACAP coverage to Brazil and the Caribbean. Baraya placed a continuing order for Brazilian publications with a well known bookseller in Rio de Janeiro in 1962, but the results fell far short of the desirable coverage. LACAP had touched only the fringe of the problem.

Brazil is a vast country—over three and a quarter million square miles in area—covering nearly half the South American continent. Although it is potentially one of the richest countries in the western hemisphere, four centuries of dependence on a single export crop—coffee—have left it poor and beset with problems such as the rising cost of living, an unfavorable balance of payments, and lack of economic and social development. Industrialization to diversify the economy is only just beginning, and communications are a major problem.

The problems of book acquisition from such an area are staggering. It was decided that before LACAP attempted to deal with them, a survey must be made by an expert who knew the book trade of Latin America and could speak Portuguese. Such a person was found in Dr. A. W. Bork, referred to earlier, who had participated in the third and subsequent Seminars. Dr. Bork had lived for twelve years in Mexico, was familiar with the book trade, and had an excellent knowledge of Spanish and Portuguese.

Starting out on May 4, 1963, Dr. Bork transacted some University business in Mexico City and Medellín, Colombia, saw Baraya in Bogotá, and did some checking for LACAP in Ecuador and Peru before reaching Pôrto Alegre, Brazil, at the end of May 1963. He had also seen the LACAP agent in Rio de Janeiro on the way. On May 31, 1963, he wrote ". . . If what I've seen so far is any indication of what is to follow, you'll be astounded at the amount of material there is to be found here." He doubted, however, from his first observations that more than 50 per cent of the São Paulo and Rio de Janeiro imprints were reaching Stechert-Hafner through their agent in Rio de Janeiro.

When the eighth Seminar met in July, 1963, Dr. Bork was still in Brazil, but he sent a report, which was supplemented a month later by a confidential report to Stechert-Hafner. In the report to the Seminar, he points out that ". . . to cover the Brazilian scene in a really competent fashion one should have four to six months" and that his study, of about six weeks' duration, was only a sampling.

It would be very difficult to summarize Dr. Bork's reports, which are filled with facts relating to the type of publishing carried on in the different centers of Brazil, particularly those outside Rio de Janeiro and São Paulo, about which very little information was available. Only some of the more general points will be mentioned here.

Speaking of publishing outside the major publishing centers in his report to the Seminar, Dr. Bork says that many influences tend to limit activity to vanity items or works of local interest. He gives the following explanation:

> Changes in the social pattern and the growth of labor unions and vocational education programs, for example, have altered the old custom of the small publisher with a fairly well organized shop in which [he] provided "apprenticeship training" to a score or more young printers under the direction of several "masters", as was mentioned by Dom Alexandre dos Santos of the at one time quite active Livraria Classica Editôra in Belém, Pará, at the mouth of the Amazon. ,

In a letter written after his return to the United States, Dr. Bork describes the difficulties of obtaining books by post from the provinces as follows:

> In my observation, the only mail which arrives with any promptness . . . is that which is sent to Pôrto Alegre, São Paulo, Rio de Janeiro and possibly Belo Horizonte. Whenever the service is irregular or the mail is picked up from one office and must pass through a second office for sorting and re-dispatch, it is delayed two or three months.

In his report to the Seminar, he says:

. . . The one great problem in Ceará is that the available transportation for the shipment of ordinary mail and parcel post is the erratic
coastwise domestic shipping, which does not seem to follow any definite
schedule or pattern. All mail from there and several of the other
capitals of coastal states (except airmail) is picked up perhaps as frequently as once a month, but often only once every two months.
. . . Five to six months' delay is common. Even airmail is erratic.
. . . Parcel post and printed matter are four or five months on their
way to the United States.

"In general," he says in his report to Stechert-Hafner, "it is about
as difficult for books from the provinces to reach the Rio de
Janeiro book market as it is for them to reach the outside world."

Mail was and is one of the main problems in communication
with Latin America. Time and again, letters from New York did
not reach Dr. Benson on her trips, or only with great delay.
Duplicate copies were often sent to her in two different cities so
what she missed in one place might catch up with her in another.
Books still arrive late, sometimes not at all. Sometimes airmail is
the only answer. Such difficulties add to the cost of the operation.

A further hazard to the book trade in Brazil noted by Dr. Bork
was inflation. He says:

With the present inflationary cycle in Brazil, the bookseller is hard
put to it to cover his payroll and current invoices. He therefore hesi-
tates to ship books . . . because payment . . . delays six months or
so . . . . In the several months which [e]lapse between invoicing and
payment, inflation eats up all the profit, and what does not disappear
in inflation is diminished by high rates of interest where money is
borrowed against accounts receivable. Twenty-four per cent interest
is a favorable rate. . . . In addition . . . banks fix high service charges
and fees and the government collects heavy taxes on transactions.

Dr. Bork points out that a bookseller always has to buy a bank
draft to pay for purchases from another city in Brazil because
checks issued on a checking account in one city are not negotiable
in another. This adds to the handling charges because he has to
pay Cr$100.00 for the draft and spend a great deal of time and
trouble to get it.

The waste of precious time has to be faced by the purchaser as
well as the bookseller. Where government or society publications

are available, exceptionally, for purchase, their actual acquisition is another problem, Dr. Bork reports. He says:

> . . . The sales office is usually open only at certain times and where more than one copy is desired, the purchaser has to secure the approval of the person in charge. This may require several trips. At times one runs onto (sic) publications of an official entity, such as the Instituto de Pesquizas Amazonicas, but is unable to run down or locate it or find out about its publications without devoting several days' time to the project.

Dr. Bork predicts that as internal transportation improves there will be a period when there is even less publishing outside the larger centers than at present. He explains why:

> . . . Places like Belém, which were formerly so isolated from the rest of the country that they almost had to do publishing on their own, now have a direct and regular land link with the larger centers of population to the south where the economically stronger publishers operate.

As can be seen, Brazil presents difficulties over and above those which exist in other Latin American countries, even Ecuador. Nevertheless, LACAP has always managed to obtain some books from that area, as the figures for the imprints received from 1960 to 1965 clearly show (see appendix I). LACAP catalog number sixteen, published in September, 1965, was devoted entirely to Brazil. It lists 2,309 titles. The increase in the number of 1963 and 1964 imprints from Brazil compared with those for 1962—588 and 732, compared with 266 for 1962—is due in large part to Dr. Bork's trip, during which he both collected information and made arrangements with booksellers, particularly in the provincial centers, for the continuing supply of current imprints. The results would have been even more appreciable if Dr. Bork had not been prevented by illness from carrying out the full program for the trip. As it was, he produced some significant results from the area which he was able to cover, and they have been duly followed up by Stechert-Hafner.

As Dr. Bork was still in Brazil when the eighth Seminar met, Coppola reported on his trip, as well as on the other LACAP activities. At the close of the discussion, the Seminar adopted the following resolution:

> That Stechert-Hafner, Inc., be commended again for its LACAP service, that congratulations be extended to the personnel involved in the project since the beginning, and that hope be expressed that it will continue to expand its coverage and to experiment with new services when feasible.

The Seminar obviously did not intend LACAP to rest on its laurels.

Recent Developments: Opening of the LACAP Office in Rio de Janeiro

It can be said that Dr. Bork's trip brought Brazil into focus for LACAP. Baraya did not visit Brazil during 1964 and 1965, but the results of the continuing orders placed by Dr. Bork were checked by Coppola from the New York office. The 1965 total for Brazilian imprints was 645. Although this was an increase over the receipts for the previous year, it was not entirely satisfactory, and Coppola had a baffled feeling that there was much more material to be had, if only he could find out about it. As so often before, bibliographic access was inadequate or lacking.

There was hope of improvement when the Library of Congress opened the first of its Latin American field offices under the National Program for Acquisitions and Cataloging in Rio de Janeiro in August, 1966. Dr. Cline reported to a committee of the American Historical Association in the Spring of 1967 that intensive bibliographical research, plus an enlarged circle of personal contracts in publishing circles, had enabled the Director of the Rio field office—Earl J. Pariseau, Assistant Director of the Hispanic Foundation—to locate a substantial number of publications, both commercial and non-commercial. Mrs. Shepard points out in her *Progress Report* to XII SALALM that, with the establishment of a LACAP office in Rio, the Library of Congress acquisitions are coordinated with those of LACAP. The official LACAP number is assigned in Rio to each publication obtained for the Program. This number is later included in the Library of Congress catalog card.

Realizing that much bibliographical information would become available as a result of the opening of the Library of Congress's Brazilian field office, and being dissatisfied with the existing arrangements for acquiring Brazilian publications, Coppola asked Baraya to go to Brazil in 1967. Baraya visited Rio de Janeiro, São Paulo, and Pôrto Alegre, and started to make the preliminary arrangements for opening the Stechert-Hafner office in Rio de Janeiro. There was much that he did accomplish, but he obviously could not spend all his time there to the neglect of the other LACAP countries. After giving the matter serious consideration Coppola decided that a Director should be appointed for the Rio office, thus releasing Baraya for other duties.

In May of 1967, Coppola, Robert S. Hafner, Executive Vice-President of Stechert-Hafner, and Robert E. Krieger, Treasurer, visited Rio de Janeiro for the official inauguration of the office. Coppola worked out the operational procedures for the new office and engaged Vicente Barretto, a young Brazilian intellectual and littérateur, to run it. Before joining Stechert-Hafner's, Barretto was the editor of *Cadernos Brasileiros,* a literary magazine, and he is therefore familiar with literary circles in Brazil. He is also familiar with American ways, for he spent some time in the United States a few years ago under one of the State Department programs. Portuguese is his native tong but he speaks English without difficulty, and Coppola found him interested and keen on the job.

Having attended the official inauguration of the office and seen Barretto installed, Coppola left Baraya to explain the new procedures and went to investigate the publishing situation in Brasilia, which had not yet been visited for LACAP. He estimates that when the Rio office is in full operation, it will be able to furnish appreciably more titles than heretofore, including many institutional publications.

CHAPTER XV

LACAP in Mid-1967

It was already clear by the end of 1965 that LACAP had achieved its goal of providing its participants with a steady flow of the printed materials published in Latin America. By mid-1967, a new office had been opened in Brazil and procurement from that country was being stepped up. A committee had been appointed, under the chairmanship of Joseph A. Rosenthal, Chief of the Preparation Division of the New York Public Library, to maintain liaison between LACAP and the Library of Congress program in Brazil, which is part of the National Program for Acquisitions and Cataloging. Participation had increased to thirty-eight, and new procedures, such as the numbering of all LACAP titles, had been introduced.

The success of LACAP was part of the broader achievements of the Seminars on the Acquisition of Latin American Library Materials, the twelfth of which was held in June, 1967. The Seminars had in fact succeeded so well in their task even three years earlier that the ninth Seminar was announced in the March 15, 1964, issue of the *Library Journal* under the heading "Pan American Union Concludes Latin American Seminar Series," and *Farmington Plan Newsletter No. 19,* published in May of the same year, carried a similar heading. This was somewhat premature, for not only have there been three more Seminars since that time, there is every indication that they will continue.

Acquisitions

The statistics of the LACAP titles for 1960 to 1965 are to be found in appendix I. As can be seen, the number of imprints for each year averages about 3,250. It is still too early to give the figures for 1966, but Coppola reported to the twelfth Seminar that the 1965 total of 3,330 was likely to be surpassed. The annual totals are given by year of imprint, not by year of receipt, so that the tables in appendix I do not indicate the actual receipts for each year. New 1960 titles, for instance, may still turn up in 1967, thus altering the 1960 total. However, as most of the titles actually reach the United States during the year in which they are published, the total imprints for a given year are close to the actual receipts. The total number of imprints has risen from 1,622, the final figure for 1960 imprints as of April, 1967, to 3,330 for 1965, the last year for which complete figures are available, with a peak of 5,309 in 1964. Except in the first year, the total has never fallen below 3,016, which reflects a period of changeover and reorganization. The total number of imprints for the six years 1960-1965 is 19,791, a respectable figure for the operation.

The LACAP receipts include books on law, medicine, agriculture, and other sciences, and some government, university and society publications, but the majority are works in the fields of literature, the humanities, and the social sciences. The proportion of literary works in the total receipts was not established, as no content analysis of the LACAP titles was undertaken, but it is certainly sizeable. Perhaps some future doctoral dissertation will establish the exact figure. In any event, it is safe to say that the LACAP receipts include many works of value to the research worker which would never have reached the United States in the normal way. The proportion of provincial publications in the total receipts is certainly higher than ever before.

The author had intended to compare the statistics of the LACAP receipts with either the total book production of the countries concerned or the Farmington Plan receipts in order to obtain a rough measurement of the Program's success, but this proved impracticable. Where book production statistics were available, they were not always comparable, because of differences of definition and periods covered, and also because of lacunae. A comparison with national bibliographies was considered but was abandoned because such bibliographies contain both retrospective and current works, and also because no sound basis could be found for selecting the bibliographies with which to make the comparison. Even an attempt to compare the holdings of a certain number of LACAP titles, as recorded in the *National Union Catalog* for 1965, with holdings of works by the same authors ten years earlier failed, owing to the nature of the *National Union Catalog* itself. It may be possible to carry out this check some years from now if the information in the *Register of Additional*

Locations is included in some future quinquennial cumulation, but it is certainly not possible at the present time.

Nevertheless, it was possible to gain some idea of the probable magnitude of the holdings of LACAP authors in 1956-1957 and of LACAP titles in 1965, even though accurate measurement was out of the question. In 1956 and 1957, there were only a few instances where the authors checked were held by any other library than the Library of Congress, and they were never held by more than three or four libraries in all. Even assuming that not all holdings were reported, they cannot have been so large as in 1965, when there are many entries showing that LACAP titles were held by a dozen and more libraries. The actual holdings are certainly very much larger.

Besides the current imprints, many out-of-print titles have been brought into the United States as a by-product of LACAP. About 2,000 current and retrospective titles are listed in each issue of *Latin America,* the LACAP catalog, and the total for the twenty-one catalogs published between December, 1960, and April, 1967, is over 37,000. If the 19,500 or so current imprints are deducted, the figure for out-of-print titles is roughly 17,500, that is to say, an average of about 2,500 a year for the seven-year period. This figure is approximate, as the total for 1966 imprints is not yet available and the periods covered by the nineteen catalogs and the figures for current imprints are not exactly the same.

Current publications were arriving so regularly that from 1963 onwards they were taken more or less for granted, and Stechert-Hafner was urged to turn its attention to other areas. It was asked by the eighth, ninth and tenth Seminars to experiment with new services, to report on periodicals that had ceased publication, and to experiment with procurement in depth of institutional publications and of serials.

Stechert-Hafner has been giving an increasing amount of thought to the procurement of government and society publications, which appear on the LACAP lists more frequently every year. Baraya paid special attention to these publications on his trip to Venezuela in 1965, with the result that there has been a notable increase in the number of publications of this type in the receipts from Venezuela over the last eighteen months. The situation has also improved considerably in Brazil, where the information on bibliographical sources assembled by the Library of Congress office in Rio de Janeiro has made it possible to obtain many hitherto inaccessible publications of this type, as well as commercial publications.

The substantial flow of Latin American titles under LACAP has not only enriched the holdings of the participating libraries, it has done something to encourage the book trade in Latin America itself. Every title found swells the total volume of business for booksellers and publishers. If a dealer supplies twelve copies of each of two hundred titles in a year, he sells 2,400 volumes, which is a large enough number to be worth his while. Thus, knowing that they have a steady market for current publications in multiple copies, booksellers in Latin America are more interested than they used to be in supplying books to the United States. Performance sometimes falls off, and some dealers are interested only in bulk orders, but the general picture is better than it was ten years ago.

Both continents gain by the improvement of the book trade. There is certainly less chance now than there was before LACAP began to operate that a book will be written in Latin America, be published, and disappear, leaving nothing but a "nostalgic rumor that such a book once was,"[1] as Vance Bourjaily puts it. And libraries with interests in Latin America are getting more of the books they want.

Costs

There are two main points to be considered in a study of costs. One is the cost of the operation itself, and the other is the cost of the books to libraries, and these two points must be considered in relation to the result obtained. Both the supplier and the libraries must ask themselves whether the benefits that accrue are worth the outlay. Any answer to this question must be largely a matter of judgment in the absence of a cost analysis. At the present time it is not possible to do more than indicate some of the factors that should be taken into account in such a study.

As to operating costs, it is obvious that LACAP cannot be an inexpensive operation. Besides the normal overheads of the New York office, some of which must be debited to the LACAP account, there are the expenses of two Latin American offices, the salaries of the traveling agent and of the head of the Brazilian office, and a considerable outlay in travel funds, hotel accommodations, and living expenses. Writing in May, 1962, before either of the Latin American offices had been opened, Dr. Benson said, "No one realizes more than I what these expenses have been nor how close you people have kept your margin of profit, if profit there has been." It was hoped that it might be possible to run the operation more economically with a permanent agent in the field, but it is probable that any savings achieved through this and a certain streamlining of procedures have been offset by an increased outlay in travel funds and related expenses. In addition to these basic expenses, there are the costs of shipping and handling, which may be high, particularly in areas where communications are difficult. In Colombia, for instance, books have to be dispatched from Bogotá by air. There are also many other incidental charges. The cost of billing, for instance, is so high that it may be more economical for a bookseller to give a volume away than bill a customer for it. Purchasers who buy in bulk—a hundred copies or more—receive substantial discounts which absorb some of these costs, but that is not the case for LACAP. The discount on purchases of twelve or even twenty copies is never very high, and it is sometimes negligible or non-existent.

The costs and a margin of profit to make the operation worthwhile are passed on to the libraries in the prices of the books. But the cost of a book is not just the cost of so much print, paper, and binding. In paying for a book purchased through LACAP, libraries are paying for a service as well. What they have to consider, therefore, is whether they could get equivalent service more cheaply, or at all. That is a matter which the libraries themselves must decide.

LACAP was launched as a commercial venture because it was felt that private enterprise encouraged by the profit motive offered a possible, permanent solution to the effective acquisition of Latin American library materials, as Kingery pointed out. However, in launching LACAP, Stechert-Hafner was concerned not only with the commercial aspects of the scheme but with the aim of service to libraries, which was in harmony with its own traditions. The relationship between those two aspects of the venture was recognized by the sixth Seminar in its resolution on the price structure of LACAP materials already quoted: "That United States libraries recognize their responsibility to support a realistic price structure for LACAP materials in order to assure the continuation of the program." Dr. Benson pointed out in her report to the sixth Seminar that libraries in the United States would receive largely the type of service they were willing to pay for and could expect no more; but it was in her report to the preceding Seminar that she went to the heart of the matter. She said, "A good commercial book firm could resolve the problem to their financial benefit only if it goes into the venture on a long-term and continuing basis and has the support of U.S. libraries."

As Stechert-Hafner is a commercial firm, it cannot be expected to act like a non-profit organization. Any library ordering books through LACAP must face that fact. On the other hand, it is fully entitled to ask, first, whether the margin of profit is too great and, secondly, whether Stechert-Hafner is operating a monopoly and charging too much. There are no records of any discussions of the first point, and it is indeed impossible to discuss it in the absence of information, but the second was the subject of some debate at the fifth Seminar, when Arthur E. Gropp, Director of the Columbus Memorial Library, raised the question in connexion with the availability of publications in Latin America. The discussion was inconclusive, but the resolution on the price structure of LACAP materials adopted by the next Seminar and the fact that now nearly forty libraries are participants in LACAP would seem to show that the danger is not considered to be too great. In the absence of comparative figures, it is impossible to make a sound judgment, but it is the writer's impression—admittedly subjective—that although LACAP certainly does not run at a loss, it is at least as much a prestige operation as it is a moneymaker.

As to the cost of the books themselves, this question was approached from the two angles of actual prices and average prices, but only in the latter case was the writer able to collect enough information to formulate valid conclusions. A rapid check of LACAP prices against those of an Argentine dealer (see appendix II, table 1) showed that there was very little difference between the two. No attempt was made to convert local prices into dollars for any of the countries because of the complications and variations in exchange rates and because the writer has no experience in this area. Instead, the LACAP lists for April and November, 1963, were checked against *Libros en Venta,* which gave dollar prices for forty out of the 466 items on the two lists. (Eighty-six Brazilian items were excluded because *Libros en Venta* does not cover Brazil). This is not a really valid comparison, as the *Libros en Venta* prices are prices paid abroad without any mark-up, and postage, handling charges, etc., must be added. The results of the check are given in appendix II, table 2, purely for information.

As was to be expected, the LACAP prices are, in general, higher than those quoted in *Libros en Venta,* but in one instance the LACAP price is 10 per cent lower. The check also showed that the LACAP floor price of $1.50 represents a much greater increase over the local price than do the prices of more expensive materials. Thus, the price of pamphlets can be considered high, but it is the price below which it is simply not an economic proposition for Stechert-Hafner to handle these materials. When these and other materials can be bought on the spot by Faculty members on vacation or library staff on buying trips, they can certainly be acquired more cheaply in terms of actual cash paid to the publisher or dealer, but that is not the price to the library. The hidden costs represented by the Faculty or staff member's travel and living expenses have to be borne in mind even when they are not directly chargeable to the library's budget. In addition, as acquisitions made by Faculty members are necessarily patchy because they depend on fortuitous circumstances, the library has to consider the cost of the materials required to round out such local purchases. Average costs, therefore, seem to be a better guide than spot comparisons of actual prices.

Even here, reliable information was not easy to come by, but Dr. Benson has provided some figures in the paper entitled "The Acquisition of Mexican Materials at the University of Texas," which she prepared for the tenth Seminar. The average price of 1963 monographis given in this paper is $3.71. The average LACAP price for 1963 Mexican imprints is $5.97, which is considerably higher. It is exceptional, however. The average LACAP prices for 1960, 1961 and 1962 Mexican imprints are $3.53, $4.04 and $4.20 respectively, and those for 1964 and 1965 are $4.82 and $4.45. The average price for all Mexican imprints acquired by LACAP from 1960-1965 (1,861 items) is $4.51. Thus, although the average LACAP price for Mexican imprints is higher than that paid by the University of Texas to its regular supplier, it is not out of all proportion.

The average prices of LACAP materials for all countries—a total of 19,791 items—are as follows:

Year of Imprint	Average Price (in US dollars)
1960	3.25
1961	3.56
1962	3.64
1963	3.97
1964	3.79
1965	4.00

The average price for all imprints 1960-1965 is $3.75. The increase from 1960 to 1965 is $0.75. The significance of this figure cannot be established without making a comparison between the LACAP prices and those of similar materials from other sources, which the writer did not attempt to do. It is safe to say, however, that the period 1960-1965 was a period of rising book prices and that the trend is continuing. The LACAP prices would therefore seem to be following the general trend.

The information on which the above calculations are based is to be found in appendix I.

Organization and Operating Procedures

LACAP is supported by the libraries which have placed blanket orders for Latin American publications. It is run from the New York office of Stechert-Hafner, Inc., where Coppola is in charge of the Program. He has an MS from the School of Library Service of Columbia University and he is responsible for the planning— the decisions as to which countries shall be visited when, for instance—and for the supervision of the day-to-day operations. He also travels on LACAP business, and represents the firm at meetings, such as those of SALALM and the American Library Association. He is assisted by Leo Cucco, who has been with the company for nearly twenty years and has worked with LACAP from the beginning; Cucco looks after much of the detail in the running of the machinery and keeps Coppola informed when he is away.

One of Coppola's most useful contributions to LACAP has been the perfecting of the records and procedures, which have been simplified and made practically foolproof. On the basis of the records kept in the New York office, it is possible to assess the performance of dealers, detect titles which have not been delivered, compile lists of new titles to be sought, etc. The records indicate whether the operation is running satisfactorily, and if not, in what area the trouble lies.

The procedure for dealing with books in the New York office is simple. As the packages arrive, they are divided into lots by country of origin, unpacked, and "cataloged," i.e., the books are identified, marked and numbered, and the entries are prepared for the LACAP lists and catalogs. The numbering is a recent innovation, having been introduced in February, 1967. All titles acquired since that time bear a distinctive number, which somewhat resembles a Library of Congress catalog number in that it is prefixed by an indication of the year, e.g., 67-1054.

All reports go to Coppola and are answered by him or his assistant. One of the fundamental factors which have made for the success of LACAP is the prompt attention which all communications receive. The action taken may be nothing more than a comment, but it is usually practical and immediate—giving instructions, settling a difficulty over payment, deciding whether or not material should be bought, for instance—and for this reason, communication between headquarters and the field is good. The LACAP agent in Bogotá does not feel cut off from the head office, although the vagaries of the mails may be a problem at times when he is on field trips. The reports are indexed, and a record is kept of all information and decisions. The Chairman of the Board is consulted on all major points and kept informed of all operations.

The operating procedures which keep LACAP running smoothly are simple and, above all, flexible. They will be considered, first, from the point of view of the participating libraries and, secondly, from that of procurement.

A library wishing to participate in LACAP places a blanket order for the publications it wishes to receive. These may be all the current imprints from all the Latin American countries or from only some of the countries. They may be books in one specific subject area, such as law or medicine, from all the countries or only from specified countries. The order is defined by the library itself, which can return unacceptable publications within certain limits.

The cost of participation varies according to the type of order. It may be quite low if the library requires materials in only one subject area or from only a few countries. It may be as high as $12,000 to $15,000 if the library requires extensive coverage of all countries. This is a substantial sum for a small library, but no small library would want full coverage, and for libraries with budgets of $250,000 or more it is not a large amount. Furthermore, it is the cost of the books only. There is no service charge.

What does the library get for its money? First, it gets current works by Latin American authors as they appear. There is no question of a book being out of print by the time it is ordered, for the books are dispatched to the libraries as soon as they arrive in New York, before they are recorded in any bibliography. The LACAP lists are published after the books have been distributed to the participating libraries. Any LACAP library which does not have an all-inclusive order and any library which is not a participant in LACAP can order materials from the LACAP lists or catalogs, but here there is a danger that a book may be out of print, or at least not in stock in New York, when it is ordered, as Stechert-Hafner buys only a limited number of copies for stock.

These are the more tangible advantages. There are others which are more difficult to assess. One is the fact a library receives titles of which it might never have heard otherwise. This is possible only because there is someone on the spot constantly seeking out new titles as they appear. Another is the saving of the library staff's time. Stechert-Hafner takes on the responsibility, not only for ordering and dispatching whatever categories of books the library has asked for, but for all negotiations and correspondence with sources abroad, which can be very time-consuming. Moreover, because of its organization and the fact that Baraya is on the spot, LACAP will get results which cannot be achieved by correspondence. Stechert-Hafner also relieves libraries of the need to deal in foreign currencies and to make arrangements dirctly with dealers and publishers in Latin America. Since LACAP is run from New York, libraries correspond only with the New York office and do not have to write in Spanish or Portuguese. Urgent instructions may be telephoned. The return of unwanted materials to New York is easy, and libraries do not have to ship returned items to sources abroad, which is always a complicated matter.

The disadvantages of this procedure, according to its critics, are: the books are too expensive; blanket orders involve an abdication of the librarian's responsibility for selection; some of the books received are not worth buying; and lastly, if the book funds are committed for a blanket order, the librarian may be unable to meet special requests for books of immediate interest. The first three points are discussed in chapter XVI and are mentioned here only *pro memoria* and to ensure a balanced presentation. As to the fourth, it is unlikely that any library would commit all its funds for blanket orders. A judicious allocation of the money available should remove or diminish this danger.

The procedure for procuring the books is not quite so simple as the blanket order but it is not unduly complicated. When Dr. Benson made her first trip, she left continuing orders with book dealers and publishers in all the towns she visited. The dealer or publisher who receives a continuing order undertakes to supply such specific categories of materials as new imprints by national authors or government and university publications, as and when they appear. This is not a simple task, as the new imprints have to be sought out and dispatched before they can go out of print, and this has to be done regularly because printings are small and soon exhausted.

This is where Baraya comes in. He travels constantly seeking out new titles, ironing out difficulties, checking performance, and keeping the New York office informed. The fact that he will be returning introduces a continuity into the relations with the suppliers which has hitherto been lacking. It is not only a matter of keeping the supplier up to the mark, however. The supplier also knows that if he has a problem, such as a delay in the settlement of his account, he can mention it to Baraya. Action follows, for one of the factors which have made for the success of LACAP is the close relationship between the head office and Bogotá. This is, of course, only sound business practice, but sound business practice has a way of misfiring in Latin America. LACAP makes it work.

Participation

In January, 1960, when Dr. Benson set out on her first trip for LACAP, the Project was assured of the support of only four libraries—the New York Public Library, the University of Texas, the University of Kansas, and the Library of Congress. The number of participants has grown steadily, and by June, 1967, it had reached thirty-eight (see appendix III, table 1). The participants include three U. S. government institutions (the Library of Congress, the National Agricultural Library, and the National Library of Medicine), two public libraries (New York and Boston), and six foreign libraries (the National Library of Australia, the Universidad del Valle, Colombia, the Universities of Alberta and Toronto, Canada, and the Universities of Essex and Sheffield, England). There were five participants from the University of California until the end of 1966, when the Bio-Medical Center at San Diego withdrew, finding selective purchasing better suited to its specialized field. The two newest participants are Pennsylvania State University and the library school of the University of Pittsburgh.

It is noteworthy that two English universities have joined the program, for English university libraries do not usually have such generous book budgets as their American counterparts. A "British Farmington Plan" was considered by the [British] Library Association after the war, but the idea was not pursued, largely because of the expense involved.[2] It has been revived, however, in a modified form and in relation to Latin America only. In its report,[3] the Committee on Latin American Studies of the [British] University Grants Committee recommended that Centres (*sic*) of Latin American Studies should be established in five universities, and that these Centres should be assisted to build adequate library collections. The Centres are located in the Universities of Cambridge, Glasgow, Liverpool, London, and Oxford. Librarians from two of these Centres participated in the eleventh Seminar.

Members of the Committee visited universities and institutions in North and South America and on their return to England they recommended, *inter alia,* that:

> University libraries making provision for Latin American studies should examine the merits of the Latin American Cooperative Acquisitions

Project in the United States for finding and purchasing books and periodicals published in Latin America.

In the body of the report, the Committee describes the Project and then adds:

> . . . It has been represented to us that perhaps 90 per cent of the material obtainable under LACP (*sic*) cannot be obtained from booksellers and that LACP has proved not only the easiest and most efficient form of procurement but also the most economical both in time and money.

All but two of the twenty-eight American university libraries which participate in LACAP are mentioned in an article by Robert B. Downs on doctoral programs and library resources in the March, 1966, issue of *College and Research Libraries*. The purpose of Dr. Downs' investigation was "to determine whether there exists any direct correlation between the number and variety of doctoral degree awarded and the strength of the library resources of individual institutions." The article is accompanied by a table in which the institutions are arranged in order of the number of doctoral degrees conferred. Dr. Downs says:

> A glance at the table . . . will reveal a close relationship, in general, between degrees and library support. Among the thirty-seven universities which awarded more than seven hundred degrees each during the decade [1953-1962] only ten had less than a million volumes, and none possessed less than half a million . . .
>
> . . . Of the 93,799 doctoral degrees awarded in the United States for the 1953-1962 period, 58,150, or nearly two-thirds, came out of thirty universities with libraries containing more than one million volumes each.

The thirty universities with holdings of more than a million volumes are shown in appendix III, table 2. Ten of these thirty universities (thirteen libraries, as the University of California has four separate participating libraries) are LACAP participants. In addition, two other LACAP participants—the University of Florida and the University of Kansas—which did not have a million volumes in 1962, the latest year to which Dr. Downs' figures relate, have now passed the million mark. Thus, nearly half the LACAP participants are libraries with a million or more volumes.

Dr. Downs recognizes that "since there are no established norms, exactly how many volumes should be held by the library and how much money should be spent for books in an institution offering doctoral programs are debatable matters," but he feels that some conclusion is possible. He says:

> . . . Pragmatically speaking, . . . it seems doubtful that high-level doctoral work in a variety of fields can be carried on with less than half a million volumes and with annual book expenditures under $200,000.

It is interesting to consider Dr. Downs' figures in the light of the statistical analysis of sixty-two ARL academic libraries carried out by the ARL in 1963.[4] This analysis shows that in 1961-1962, the total holdings of sixty-two ARL academic libraries were 82,803,809 volumes, and their total budget for books, periodicals and binding was $23,799,675.00, that is to say, an average of 1,337,558 volumes and $383,865.00 for each library. The figures are not strictly comparable, as Dr. Downs does not indicate whether his $200,000 includes expenditure for periodicals and binding. Presumably it does not, or the fact would have been mentioned. Nevertheless, the ARL analysis shows that Dr. Downs' figures are, if anything, an under-estimate. Both sets of figures are, however, indicative of the magnitude of research collections in the United States. It is against this background that LACAP must be seen.

Only two of the LACAP libraries mentioned in Dr. Downs' article fall seriously below the standard he sets, and seventeen are substantially above it. Thus it can be seen that the LACAP participants are, on the whole, the large libraries with ample budgets. Full participation is not for small libraries, although limited participation, restricted to one or more countries or subject areas, is within the reach of the smaller libraries. The Program may not be suitable for special libraries either, as selection is a paramount consideration in their case. Nevertheless, for the libraries that can afford it, LACAP is probably "not only the easiest and most efficient form of procurement, but also the most economical in time and money," a possibility mentioned in the Parry Report.

LACAP—An Imaginative Venture

Publications and Contribution to Bibliography

Between June, 1960, and April, 1967, Stechert-Hafner published forty-nine LACAP lists—*New Latin American Books*. The most recent list is, however, numbered only 48, because there are two lists 1, one published in June, 1960, and distributed at the fifth Seminar, and the second, starting the regular series, in September, 1962. Over the same period twenty-one catalogs—*Latin America*—were published, and three special lists of LACAP materials—*Latin American Periodicals* (1961), *Latin American Law* (1962), and *Books from the Caribbean* (1963). The most recent catalog is devoted entirely to materials from Brazil. In addition, some LACAP materials are included in the catalog *Spanish and Hispanic American Literature*.

Both the lists and the catalogs are attractively presented, the lists with a distinctive blue masthead and the catalogs in covers of clear, bright colors, which vary with each issue. The entries are carefully prepared and well printed and are easy to read and use. The titles are arranged alphabetically by country and by author under each country in both the lists and the catalogs, and some of the recent catalogs have been further sub-classified by subject. The catalogs have a useful country index inside the front cover.

The contribution to bibliography made by the LACAP lists and catalogs has already been mentioned in chapter IV and need not be discussed again. Suffice it to say that the listing of nearly 20,000 new titles over a period of slightly more than seven years is a substantial contribution.

LACAP also made an indirect contribution to *Fichero Bibliográfico Hispanoamericano* in the early days. Originally, some of the material for *Fichero* was taken from the cataloging done by the New York Public Library. As the Library was a participant in the Project, it received most of its Latin American materials through LACAP, which thus provided some of the bibliographical material for *Fichero*. This is no longer so, however, as *Fichero* is now prepared by the Bowker office in Buenos Aires.

Recapitulation

The two world wars and the studies undertaken prior to the initiation of the Farmington Plan showed there were serious gaps in the Latin American holdings of United States libraries and that a systematic plan of collecting was needed. Procurement from Latin America had proved particularly difficult and it was soon clear, from discussions in SALALM and elsewhere, notably ARL, that the only way to improve it was by solving some of the problems of the Latin American book trade. These problems were attacked by the Farmington Plan, on the one hand, through its Subcommittee on Latin American Resources, and by Stechert-Hafner, through LACAP, on the other.

There can be no doubt that LACAP has greatly improved the coverage of Latin American imprints by American research libraries. Through a technique which consists essentially in search and supervision by a traveling agent, the participating libraries have received nearly 20,000 current titles, and over 17,000 retrospective titles have been made available to them. The location of new titles by Latin American authors before they could go out of print has enabled libraries to build more balanced Latin American collections. The geographical coverage is the most complete ever achieved. Not only are all the major countries of Latin America covered, including Central America and the Caribbean, but the publications of the provinces are covered as well as those of the capitals. Cuba is the only country not included in LACAP, but some of its publications are obtained through other countries. Although no means of measuring the actual extent of LACAP's coverage was found, it is clear that a greater proportion of the Latin American book production is now covered than was possible ten years ago. Although many libraries have satisfactory arrangements with dealers in different Latin American countries, no library has satisfactory arrangements with all of them except through LACAP. The libraries are not only learning of books before they have been recorded in any bibliography, they are getting the books themselves.

The blanket order procedure employed by LACAP is not only an efficient means of achieving systematic coverage, it is probably also the most economical in time and money. Provided a library is large enough to envisage collecting on an all-inclusive scale, the blanket order is the obvious means to ensure the required flow of books. On the whole, it is not a procedure for small libraries, unless they restrict their orders to specific countries or subject areas, but for the larger libraries it achieves a saving of staff time and therefore of money. In addition, because it comes as near to complete coverage as is humanly possible, it is a procedure which must be adopted by librarians who are responsible for first-class research collections. As unwanted materials can be returned within reasonable limits, there is no question of "trash" being forced on participating libraries, and the receipt of such materials has its usefulness in informing the library of what is being produced. The blanket order therefore gives a better picture of what is being published than can possibly be gained by selective methods. For this reason, the books coming in through LACAP are invaluable for research purposes. They prove that two knotty problems have been solved: how to find out what is being published in Latin America, and how to obtain it. Thousands of titles have been rescued from oblivion and safely housed in libraries in the United States. This is a solid achievement which commands respect.

What of the future?

The writer had expected that when the Library of Congress launched its National Program for Acquisitions and Cataloging and opened an office in Rio de Janeiro, it would be withdrawing from LACAP or restricting its participation to a few areas. This does not seem to be the case, however. Partly because of the source of its funds—Title II-C of the Higher Education Act, 1965 —and partly because of its own traditions, the Library of Congress is placing the accent on cataloging. The National Acquisitions Plan drafted by Stanley West, which would have enabled other libraries to participate in the Library of Congress program, has been shelved. LACAP is cooperating closely with the Library of Congress, and it is probably through LACAP that libraries can most easily obtain copies of the Library of Congress's acquisitions under the new program.

Other libraries will probably be joining LACAP, and some may be leaving it. Over the past year, for instance, five new libraries have joined—three American (Ohio State, Pennsylvania State, and the library school of the University of Pittsburgh) and two foreign (the University of Alberta and the National Library of Australia) —and three have withdrawn, mainly because their needs were small. Nevertheless, LACAP is extending its membership, not only in the United States but abroad. Besides the two new foreign participants already mentioned, the University of Toronto, Canada, has joined within the last two years, and the Universidad del Valle, Colombia, and the University of Sheffield, England, have been participants since before 1965. Other foreign institutions have shown an interest in LACAP also, but the bulk of the LACAP participants will continue to be in the large United States libraries with special interests in Latin America.

It is the writer's considered view that, because of the flexibility of its procedures and the efficiency with which it is run, LACAP has come to stay. It may have competitors and imitators, but these are the measure of its success. And it will always have been a pioneer in a notoriously intractable area.

CHAPTER XVI

The Value of Books

The study of a program such as LACAP leads inevitably to a consideration of cooperative acquisitions in general, and of the blanket order procedure in particular.

If the large research libraries of the United States understand and accept, to quote Jerrold Orne, "the national responsibility for acquisition, on a global basis, of the printed record," (and there is no doubt they do accept it) they cannot escape cooperative acquisition and blanket ordering. As Eric Moon points out in the *Library Journal* of October 1, 1960, "To select when unnecessary is wasteful and stupid." For a library aiming at "complete coverage" selection is not only unnecessary, it is impossible.

"Complete coverage" is a chimera. Even those who advocate it and strive for it know it cannot be achieved. The Farmington Plan, for instance, which aims at the most comprehensive coverage of any cooperative acquisitions scheme, excludes a list of materials which takes up a whole page in the 1961 *Handbook*. Libraries cannot acquire all of the immense flood of printed matter which issues from the presses every year, and they would not be able to store it if they could. After describing the production of scientific literature, in *Libraries in the World,* IFLA states categorically, ". . . With such an avalanche of literature it is impossible even for the largest libraries to pursue the ideal of completeness."

The value of a cooperative acquisitions project lies, therefore, not in complete coverage but in the planning and the representativeness of the acquisitions. Edwin E. Williams' study, "Research Library Acquisitions from Eight Countries," published in the *Library Quarterly* in October 1945, showed that unplanned acquisitions resulted in inadequate coverage of some national and subject areas and duplication in others. Clapp[1] and Boyd,[2] among many others, have drawn attention to the dangers which such inadequacies involve for the national security. In England, Professor R. S. Hutton, Professor Emeritus of Metallurgy, Cambridge University, and a founder member of Aslib, and Lionel McColvin, are among those who have pointed out the need for planning and urged specialization.

If complete coverage cannot be achieved, what should a research library aim at in collecting? The answer will depend on the library. As Professor Hutton points out in an unpublished letter, in its own field, a library must seek as wide and as deep a coverage as possible while avoiding duplication with the holdings of other libraries in related fields. It must strive to meet the needs of its users, not only in the present but in the future, and it must ensure that its funds and its staff's time are used to the best advantage. The only way that this can be achieved is by intelligent use of the blanket order. As Rolland E. Stevens, Professor of the University of Illinois Graduate School of Library Science, says:

> . . . When a librarian learns that all imprints of a given publisher, or all works having potential significance for research are encompassed within the recognized needs of his library, does not common sense urge him to contract for a blanket order for these imprints?[3]

There are, nevertheless, objections to the blanket order. Its critics maintain that: it is expensive; it involves the abdication of the librarian's responsibility for selection; and the books received include "trash."

Collecting on the scale envisaged by Dr. Orne and the framers of the Farmington Plan can be undertaken only by the large libraries, and public institutions such as the Library of Congress. Would it be cheaper for these libraries to employ staff to select the books they need? Obviously not. If a library is collecting on a massive scale, blanket orders save both time and money, a view presented for consideration in the Parry Report.[4]

The abdication of the librarian's responsibility for selection is a more debatable point. If the librarian were to interpret his responsibility in the narrow sense, he could never delegate any part of it to anyone, which would be absurd. He must delegate responsibility if the library is to be served, and if his library is collecting on a large scale, he has no choice but to exercise his responsibility, in part, through blanket orders. He is still responsible for defining the criteria of the blanket order, supervising its operation, and modifying it as may be necessary.

The question of "trash" is extremely difficult. "Trash" may be defined roughly as "material which is useless to a particular library." What is useless to one library, however, will be valuable to another, and what is rejected today may be of value to some future research worker. Conversely, what is prized by a library today may be rejected by the same library tomorrow. If all libraries select only the important books and neglect the others, there will be whole areas which are not covered at all, as Williams and Clapp have pointed out in the articles already mentioned. This is a greater danger than the presence of a certain amount of low-grade material.

In any event, the low-grade material is of value in at least two areas. It may indicate the mentality of the culture which produced it, and it may contain valuable information not to be found elsewhere. The first case has been put very cogently by Boyd in the article already quoted, in which he argues that the publications of Nazi Germany have their value for scholarly research. Even the shoddiest of Nazi literature, he feels, may be of considerable importance to the psychologist, the historian, and to many other specialists in the lower reaches of the human mind. Nazi literature is perhaps a special case, but if the aim of research is to get at the truth—about historical events, about a culture, or anything else—the superficial and ephemeral material must be taken into account as well as what is valuable and lasting.

The second point has been dealt with by Dr. S. C. Bradford in a definitive article published in *Engineering*,[5] to which Professor Hutton kindly drew the writer's attention. In a masterly analysis, Dr. Bradford demonstrates the remarkable scatter of worthwhile articles through the whole range of technical journals. Taking the journals in two specific fields, Dr. Bradford shows that although the standard journals provide the largest number of references per journal, a substantial number of important references appear in journals where they would hardly be expected. He says, "We can only draw the conclusion that a large number of references are produced by sources which, *a priori*, are 'unlikely'." These are the sources which would probably be included in the category of "trash" because they do not often contain anything of value.

Professor Hutton makes another point. In another letter, he draws attention to the fact that articles, pamphlets, and other publications on the application of science, which are often discarded after a year or two, contain valuable and sometimes irreplaceable information. He says:

> . . . I have come across several cases of inventions in use for many years in one country and quite unknown in another whereas diligent search showed that the records were published in their early days.
>
> Another outstanding example is the energy and thoroughness with which the Russians are searching out and accumulating trade literature of foreign countries and using it to stimulate the installation of corresponding developments in their country.

This argument applies more to scientific than to literary materials, but a research library needs both.

If a library is pursuing the ideal of completeness in the literary field, it must acquire many works of new authors sight unseen, as it were. As Dr. Benson points out in her report to the fifth Seminar, promising young authors may be regarded as insignificant and their works not acquired unless someone learns that they *are* promising. In many cases, it is impossible to tell from an author's first works whether he will go far or not. The insignificant writer may be a future Balzac, and the promising young genius nothing but a sorry hack. The only solution is to acquire, if not all, as many of such works as possible.

Dr. Benson puts this point in her own way in the above-mentioned report:

> It seems to me that libraries, especially those who class themselves as research libraries in the Latin American field, are going to have to take the works of some unpromising young authors along with the promising if they expect to obtain the coverage they talk about. Who knows but what some of these young authors may turn out to be other Gabriela Mistrals.

LACAP is concerned with scientific literature and with ensuring the widest possible coverage of all works by national authors in Latin America. Naturally, the quality of the works will be uneven. If nothing but works of lasting value were selected, supposing that were possible, the collections in American libraries would give only a distorted view of the cultures they are trying to reflect. Under a cooperative acquisitions scheme such as the Farmington Plan, or LACAP, the libraries may not get everything that appears, and they may not like all they get, but their acquisitions will be more representative of what is being produced than they could be on the basis of selection. If Dr. Downs is right and there is a direct correlation between library resources and doctoral degrees, the scholars of the future will be best served by those libraries which are now participants in cooperative acquisition schemes.

Appendix I

ACQUISITIONS

Number of LACAP titles by Year and Cost*

Country	1960 Imprints	Cost	1961 Imprints	Cost	1962 Imprints	Cost
Argentina	100	$290.75	614	$2,357.75	690	$2,674.75
Bolivia	103	381.35	182	823.25	165	639.75
Brazil	378	932.80	325	829.00	266	967.00
Chile	209	829.80	312	1,097.75	400	1,251.75
Colombia	20	79.75	239	1,025.50	212	802.50
Costa Rica	13	47.50	16	66.60	34	112.75
Cuba	2	8.75	8	37.75	22	102.50
Dominican Rep.	13	54.50	6	33.00	26	95.50
Ecuador	128	375.24	185	525.25	119	369.00
French Guiana	—	—	—	—	—	—
Guatemala	28	116.50	42	130.25	49	196.25
Guyana	4	8.50	—	—	1	5.00
Haiti	15	54.75	25	83.50	30	109.75
Honduras	3	8.00	2	4.50	—	—
Jamaica	10	21.25	15	31.25	7	27.00
Mexico	225	793.90	247	997.25	279	1,172.25
Nicaragua	16	73.15	35	121.00	16	78.25
Panama	42	149.90	36	108.75	38	100.00
Paraguay	12	45.00	73	236.25	56	223.00
Peru	213	613.95	259	853.97	150	635.85
Puerto Rico	12	47.30	25	84.00	32	136.00
El Salvador	27	69.65	42	106.50	36	80.75
Surinam	3	5.25	7	10.50	.7	19.50
Trinidad and Tobago	—	—	7	12.00	6	12.00
Uruguay	12	77.50	271	825.75	170	520.25
Venezuela	34	190.50	285	1,184.50	205	632.35
Total	1,622	$5,275.54	3,258	$11,585.82	3,016	$10,963.70

* This table is based on information supplied to the XI and XII SALALM, which is used here with the permission of the Permanent Secretary of SALALM. The figures have been updated to April, 1967.

Number of LACAP Titles by Year and Cost (cont.)

Country	1963 Imprints	Cost	1964 Imprints	Cost	1965 Imprints	Cost
Argentina	860	$3,012.05	1,215	$4,094.80	737	$2,559.68
Bolivia	142	708.75	245	1,023.25	115	542.50
Brazil	588	2,372.25	732	2,746.75	645	2,190.75
Chile	210	888.50	362	1,441.25	246	1,495.74
Colombia	257	1,073.75	510	2,148.75	198	935.50
Costa Rica	41	162.75	44	214.00	14	62.50
Cuba	50	259.00	43	218.50	8	34.75
Dominican Rep.	19	73.50	9	36.00	1	1.50
Ecuador	122	301.50	297	859.75	121	347.75
French Guiana	—	—	—	—	—	—
Guatemala	71	259.50	149	781.75	164	844.50
Guyana	5	17.75	31	117.50	—	—
Haiti	18	51.00	35	96.75	11	44.25
Honduras	7	21.75	18	59.72	8	22.00
Jamaica	15	54.75	58	126.00	3	8.25
Mexico	209	1,247.50	465	2,241.50	436	1,939.00
Nicaragua	13	35.25	14	47.50	—	—
Panama	35	87.75	75	212.25	19	58.00
Paraguay	35	133.25	85	346.75	47	156.75
Peru	129	618.25	193	880.75	98	450.75
Puerto Rico	37	179.75	28	102.00	27	112.25
El Salvador	24	54.50	21	53.50	13	27.00
Surinam	6	22.00	14	36.00	2	4.50
Trinidad and Tobago	—	—	2	5.75	2	3.00
Uruguay	180	610.50	221	695.00	164	520.50
Venezuela	183	664.75	443	1,528.00	251	964.15
Total	3,256	$12,910.30	5,309	$20,113.77	3,330	$13,325.57

Appendix II

PRICES OF LACAP MATERIALS

TABLE 1

Comparison of LACAP Prices with Prices given by Fernando García Cambeiro

	FGC* $	LACAP $
1. Allende, Oscar. Punto de partida.	3.50	4.50
2. Bermann, Gregorio. La crisis argentina.	1.20	1.50
3. Cordero, Héctor Adolfo. Los valores humanos.	2.00	1.75
4. Frondizi, Arturo. Estrategia y táctica del movimiento nacional.	2.50	2.75
5. Gilberti, Horacio, et al. Sociedad, economía y reforma agraria.	1.60	1.75
6. Di Tella, Torcuato S. Socialismo en la Argentina . . .?	1.00	1.50
7. Rebollo Paz, León. La guerra del Paraguay.	2.50	2.50
8. Vargas Llosa, Marco. Los jefes.	2.00	2.25
9. Peña Lillo, Arturo. Los encantadores de serpientes.	1.50	1.50
10. Bernard, Tomás Diego. Temas de derecho e historia notarial.	2.70	2.50
11. Fortuny, Pablo. Supersticiones calchaquies.	3.50	2.75
12. Regoli de Mullen, Alicia. El mundo de los otros.	1.50	1.50
13. Dimase, Leonardo et al. La situación gremial en la Argentina.	1.00	1.50
14. Abella Caprile, Margarita. Obras completas.	5.00	4.50
15. Covadlo, Eduardo L. Los humaneros.	2.50	3.00
16. Esterkind, Beatriz. Con el ángel a cuestas.	1.20	1.50
17. Etchenique, Nira. Diez puntos.	1.40	1.50
18. Sáenz, Dalmiro A. El pecado necessario.	2.50	2.00
19. Ferrari Amores, Alfonso. A la sombra del alto manzano.	1.00	1.50

* Taken from *Monthly News Service*, March 1965—3.

Table 2

Comparison of the Prices of Forty LACAP Items* with Dollar
Prices Listed in *Libros en Venta***

	LEV $	LACAP $
Argentina		
1. Altamira, P. G. Principios de lo contencioso-administrativo.	2.00	2.50
2. Belaúnde, C. H. La economía social según Pío XII y Juan XXIII.	1.70	2.00
3. Goldstein, R. Diccionario de derecho penal.	8.00	8.50
4. Mondolfo, R. La conciencia moral de Homero a Demócrito y Epicuro.	0.55	1.50
5. Orione, J. Introducción a la humanología.	1.60	2.00
6. Alberdi, J. B. Historia de la guerra del Paraguay.	1.50	2.85
7. Atchabahian, A. & Massier, G. Régimen legal de la contabilidad pública nacional.	2.50	3.50
8. Bullaude, J. El nuevo mundo de la imagen.	0.40	1.50
9. Escardo, F. La sociedad ante el niño.	1.40	1.50
10. Franco, L. La hembra humana.	2.10	3.00
11. Iglesias Janeiro, J. Tu entrarás en el reino.	3.00	3.75
12. Iriarte, T. de—Gandia, E. de, ed. Memorias del General Iriarte.	10.88	13.00
13. León Portilla, M. Imagen del México antiguo.	0.35	1.50
14. Lewin, B. La insurrección de Tupac Amaru.	0.35	1.50
15. López, H. H. Memorias de un esquizofrénico.	1.30	2.25
16. Paso, L. De la Colonia a la Independencia Nacional	1.70	2.50
17. Roca, J. A. El General Roca y su época.	1.80	2.50
18. Sánchez Garrido, A. La lengua materna en la escuela secundaria.	0.40	1.50
19. Solari, A. E. Sociología rural latinoamericana	0.35	1.50
20. Vega, C. El Himno Nacional Argentino.	0.35	1.50

---

* Taken from LACAP Lists Nos. 6 and 10, April and November, 1963.

** The dollar prices in *Libros en Venta* are not the cost to the library, as they do not include postage and handling charges or overheads. The comparison with the LACAP prices, which are the cost of the books delivered to the library, is therefore only very rough.

TABLE 2 (cont.)

Chile

21.	Alone. Leer y escribir.	1.60	3.25
22.	Bunster, E. Motín en Punta Arenas.	2.00	5.00
23.	Coloane, F. El camino de la ballena.	1.80	3.25
24.	Castro, B.¿ Me permite una interrupción?	1.70	3.25
25.	Donoso, J. Coronación.	1.80	3.50
26.	Durand, L. Paisajes y gentes de Chile.	1.60	2.50
27.	Ferrero, M. Premios Nacionales de literatura. v.1.	1.90	3.50
28.	Garafulic, J. Quedamos en eso . . .	1.80	3.25
29.	Palazuelos, J. A. Según el orden del tiempo.	1.60	3.25
30.	Rafide, M. Poetas españoles contemporáneos.	3.50	5.75
31.	Rojas, M. Antología autobiográfica.	2.00	3.75
32.	Yáñez, M. F. ¿Dónde está el trigo y el vino?	1.60	2.50

Paraguay

33.	Pla, J. El grabado en el Paraguay.	2.00	2.75

Peru

34.	Martínez Pizarro, J. Sol interior, Mejía	0.60	
	Rama Florida	1.00	1.50
35.	Ramírez Otalora, J. Codificación de la legislación		
	de trabajo . . . en el Perú.	16.00	20.00

Venezuela

36.	Acosta Saignes, M. Estudios de folklore venezolano.	2.65	2.25
37.	Maza Zavala, D. F. Aspectos del desarrollo		
	económico de Venezuela.	1.10	1.50
38.	————————————. Problemas de la economía exterior		
	de Venezuela.	5.50	8.25
39.	Navarro Sotillo, P. La publicidad en Venezuela.	0.65	1.50
40.	Rosas Marcano, J. El terremoto del Jueves Santo.	0.35	1.50

Appendix III

PARTICIPATION

TABLE 1

Participation in LACAP as of June 1, 1967

1. Boston Public Library
2. Columbia University
3. Cornell University
4. Duke University
5. Joint Universities
6. Library of Congress
7. National Agricultural Library
8. National Library of Australia
9. National Library of Medicine
10. New York Public Library
11. Ohio State University
12. Pennsylvania State University
13. Saint Louis University
14. Stanford University
15. State University of New York at Buffalo
16. Tulane University
17. Universidad del Valle, Cali, Colombia
18. University of Alberta
19. University of Arizona
20. University of California, Berkeley, Bancroft Library
21. University of California, Berkeley, General Library
22. University of California, Los Angeles
23. University of California, Santa Barbara
24. University of Connecticut
25. University of Essex, England
26. University of Florida
27. University of Illinois
28. University of Kansas
29. University of Miami, Florida
30. University of Pittsburgh
31. University of Sheffield, England
32. University of Southern California
33. University of Texas
34. University of Toronto
35. University of Wisconsin, Madison
36. University of Wisconsin, Milwaukee
37. Washington State University, Pullman, Washington
38. Washington University, St. Louis, Missouri

TABLE 2

Library Holdings and Expenditures of Thirty-two Institutions,
1953-1962[a]

Institution[b]	LACAP[c]	Total No. of Degrees 1953-1962	Expenditure 1962	Number of volumes 1962	1964[d]
Columbia	L	5,644	$ 588,846	3,026,464	3,088,460
California (all campuses)	L	5,024	2,844,697	5,279,404	6,845,299
Wisconsin (Madison)	L	3,733	544,918	1,527,432	1,445,521[e]
Illinois	L	3,502	810,445	3,525,820	3,634,643[f]
Harvard		3,192	1,023,889	6,931,293	
Michigan		2,981	627,514	3,049,715	
N. Y. Univ.		2,870	214,446	1,150,000	
Ohio State	L	2,559	423,879	1,520,597	1,591,346
Chicago		2,363	457,213	2,210,062	
Minnesota		2,353	603,345	2,072,285	
Cornell	L	2,202	684,283	2,278,046	2,413,369
Yale		2,141	781,765	4,572,893	
Indiana		1,990	571,812	1,828,982	
Stanford	L	1,938	437,628	2,287,332	2,377,780
Iowa		1,570	337,180	1,096,996	
Texas	L	1,521	1,242,171	1,508,262	1,578,490
Pennsylvania		1,486	493,247	1,744,680	
So. California	L	1,413	222,583	1,007,891	1,052,942
Northwestern		1,336	361,774	1,666,200	
Princeton		1,137	347,343	1,754,580	
Univ. of Washington		1,124	437,125	1,173,496	
Pittsburgh		1,051	248,809	1,021,343	
North Carolina		929	425,589	1,283,109	
Johns Hopkins		905	198,785	1,207,346	
Florida	L	795	317,924	970,429	1,017,405
Missouri		787	376,669	1,043,330	
Rutgers		779	309,778	1,017,765	
Duke	L	732	470,416	1,540,062	1,592,672
Kansas	L	651	344,771	962,849	1,018,347
Louisiana		576	451,233	1,042,218	
Virginia		454	193,872	1,155,488	
Brown		444	214,619	1,170,755	

For footnotes, see next page.

Footnotes to table 2

a This table is based on Robert B. Downs, "Doctoral Programs and Library Resources." *College and Research Libraries* XXVII (March, 1966), table 1, pp.
  124-125. The information is reproduced here by courtesy of the Editor.

b The institutions were selected as follows: all the institutions on Dr. Downs' list
  with holdings of a million or more volumes in 1962 were included, and to these
  were added two LACAP participants, Florida and Kansas, which had more than
  a million volumes in 1964.

c Participants in LACAP are marked "L."

d The figures, for LACAP libraries only, are taken from the *American Library
  Directory*. 24th ed. New York: R. R. Bowker Company, 1964.

e The apparent decline in the holdings from 1962 to 1964 is due to a difference in
  reporting. For some years, the library of the University of Wisconsin, Milwaukee,
  was considered to be part of the library of the University of Wisconsin, Madison,
  and so reported. The breakdown is as follows:

	University of Wisconsin,	University of Madison Milwaukee	Wisconsin, Total
July 1, 1962	1,372,984	154,448	1,527,432
July 1, 1963	1,445,521	194,113	1,639,634

Information supplied by Gerhard B. Naeseth, Associate Director, Memorial
Library, University of Wisconsin, Madison.

f Books only. The library also contains 513,980 pamphlets.

Appendix IV

LIST OF THE

SEMINARS ON THE ACQUISITION OF LATIN AMERICAN
LIBRARY MATERIALS

I SALALM	Chinsegut Hill, Brooksville, Florida June 14-15, 1956.
II SALALM	Austin, Texas, June 19-20, 1957.
III SALALM	Berkeley, California, July 10-11, 1958.
IV SALALM	Washington, D. C., June 18-19, 1959.
V SALALM	New York City, June 14-16, 1960.
VI SALALM	Carbondale, Illinois, July 6-8, 1961.
VII SALALM	Coral Gables, Florida, June 14-16, 1962.
VIII SALALM	Madison, Wisconsin, July 11-12, 1963.
IX SALALM	St. Louis, Missouri, June 25-26, 1964.
X SALALM	Detroit, Michigan, July 1-3, 1965.
XI SALALM	Columbia University, New York City, July 7-9, 1966.
XII SALALM	University of California, Los Angeles, June 22-24, 1967.

Notes

CHAPTER I

1. The author is indebted to Mrs. Edith C. Wise, of the General University Library of New York University, for valuable help with the first part of this chapter.

CHAPTER III

1. William H. Kurth, "The Acquisition of Research Materials from South America: A Preliminary Report." In: "Report of the Cooperative Library Mission to Latin America (September-December, 1958), Including Field Reports." Washington: Library of Congress, 1959. Photo-offset. Separately paged. 13 pp.

CHAPTER IV

1. This chapter is largely based on information contained in Mrs. Shepard's Progress Reports to XI and XII SALALM, "A Report of Bibliographic Activities, 1965 . . . ," by Carl W. Deal, and "A Report on the Hispanic Foundation's Bibliographic Activities Related to Latin America, 1965-1966," by Earl J. Pariseau, both submitted to XI SALALM, and on the *Annual Report* of the Librarian of Congress for the years ending June 30, 1965 and June 30, 1966.

2. The author is again indebted to Mrs. Wise for valuable help with the first part of this chapter.

3. Marietta Daniels Shepard, "The Inter-American Program for Library and Bibliographic Development of the Organization of American States." *Libri* XII (1962), pp. 139-145.

4. The National Program for Acquisitions and Cataloging is the outcome of several years of planning. As soon as it became clear that funds would be available for strengthening college and research library resources under Title II-C of the Higher Education Act, 1965, planning began. Stanley West, who had been concerned with acquisitions from Latin America for many years, most recently as Chairman of the Farmington Plan Subcommittee on Latin American Resources, was engaged as consultant by the Library of Congress in 1964 and asked to draft a national acquisitions scheme, known as the National Acquisitions Plan. He was thinking in terms of some kind of cooperative arrangement for acquisitions, but with a strong emphasis on cataloging. He drafted two plans, which were submitted to the Library of Congress in January and in March, 1965, but both were overtaken by events for 1966 saw the launching of the National Program for Acquisitions and Cataloging (NPAC).

Title II-C of the Higher Education Act, 1965, authorized an appropriation of $5 million for the fiscal year ending June 30, 1966, $6,315,000 for the following year, and $7,770,000 for 1967-1968. It also authorized the Commissioner of Education to transfer funds to the Librarian of Congress for the acquisition and prompt cataloging of library materials currently published throughout the world. It was thus that the Shared Cataloging Program came into being and the

Library of Congress set up its new Shared Cataloging Division. After an important conference at the British Museum in January, 1966, attended by representatives of the Library of Congress and important European libraries, the first experiment in shared cataloging got under way in London in April, 1966. The Library of Congress received advance copy of the *British National Bibliography* and current British imprints through a combination of blanket ordering and selection. The first NPAC overseas office for shared cataloging was opened in London in June and the second one in Paris in November. Others are being opened in Oslo, Vienna, and Wiesbaden. In the meantime, the Library of Congress has opened two field offices, one in Nairobi and the other in Rio de Janeiro. The field office in Rio de Janeiro, which is considered here in relation to acquisitions from Latin America, must be viewed as part of the worldwide NPAC to be seen in its true perspective.

(This account has been compiled from information supplied by Stanley West and from the *Annual Reports* of the Librarian of Congress for the years ending June 30, 1966 and June 30, 1967).

CHAPTER V

1. T. R. Barcus and Verner W. Clapp, "Collecting in the National Interest." *Library Trends* III (April, 1955), pp. 337-355.

2. Robert B. Downs, "Wartime Co-operative Aquisitions." *Library Quarterly* XIX (July, 1949), pp. 157-165.

3. Julian P. Boyd, "A Landmark in the History of Library Cooperation . . ." *College and Research Libraries* VIII (April, 1947), pp. 101-109.

4. Henry T. Drennan, "Cooperative Selection and Book Ordering." In: *Selection and Acquisition Procedures in Medium-Sized and Large Libraries.* Herbert Goldhor, ed. Champaign, Illinois: The Illini Union Bookstore, 1963, pp. 55-70.

5. Robert B. Downs, "Library Cooperation and Specialization." In: *Problems and Prospects of the Research Library.* Association of Research Libraries. Edwin E. Williams, ed. New Brunswick, N. J.: The Scarecrow Press, 1955, pp. 91-104.

6. Robert Vosper, *The Farmington Plan Survey* . . . University of Illinois Graduate School of Library Science. Occasional Papers. No. 77. October, 1965. Urbana, Illinois: University of Illinois Graduate School of Library Science [1965]

7. Keyes D. Metcalf and Edwin E. Williams, "Proposal for a Division of Responsibility among American Libraries in the Acquisition and Recording of Library Materials." *College and Research Libraries* V (March, 1944), pp. 105-109.

8. William H. Kurth, "Report of the Cooperative Library Mission to Latin America . . ." Washington: Library of Congress, 1959.

CHAPTER VI

1. Vosper, *op. cit.,* p. 3.

2. Edwin E. Williams, *Farmington Plan Handbook, Revised to 1961 and Abridged.* [Cambridge, Mass.] Association of Research Libraries, 1961, pp. 21, 23.

CHAPTER XI

1. Later Assistant Vice-President in charge of operations in Latin America.

CHAPTER XV

1. Vance Bourjaily, "The Lost Books of Latin America." *Publishers Weekly* CLXXVII (April 11, 1960) , pp. 14-15.

2. "Co-operative Provision of Books, Periodicals and Related Materials, in Libraries." Final Report of the Sub-Committee on the Co-operative Provision of Books . . . *Library Association Record* LIX (July, 1957) , pp. 235-237.

3. University Grants Committee, *Report of the Committee on Latin American Studies.* London: Her Majesty's Stationery Office, 1965 [Parry Report]

4. "Statistical Analysis of Sixty-two ARL Academic Libraries 1951-52—1961-62." Association of Research Libraries. *Minutes of the Sixty-third Meeting* . . . *January 26, 1964, Chicago, Illinois,* appendix D, p. 47.

CHAPTER XVI

1. Verner W. Clapp, "The Balance of Conflicting Interests in Building Collections —Comprehensiveness versus Selectivity." In: *Changing Patterns of Scholarship and the Future of Research Libraries* . . . Philadelphia: University of Pennsylvania Press, 1951, pp. 65-72.

2. Boyd, *op. cit.*

3. Rolland E. Stevens, "No Librarian Will Defend a 'Get-'Em-All' Theory." In: "The 'Get-'Em-All' Theory of Book Buying." *Library Journal* LXXXV (October 1, 1960) , p. 3392.

4. University Grants Committee, *op. cit.*

5. S. C. Bradford, "Sources of Information on Specific Subjects." *Engineering* (January 26, 1934) . British Society for International Bibliography. Publication Number 1.

Short Selected Bibliography

Aguilera, Francisco, Benjamin, Curtis, and Lacy, Dan. *Books in Latin America*. New York: Franklin Publications, Inc., 1962.

Association of Research Libraries. *Problems and Prospects of the Research Library*. Edwin E. Williams, ed. New Brunswick, N. J.: The Scarecrow Press, 1955.

Barcus, T. R., and Clapp, Verner W. "Collecting in the National Interest." *Library Trends* III (April, 1955), pp. 337-355.

Barker, R. E. *Books for All: A Study of the International Book Trade*. [Paris] UNESCO, 1956.

Benson, Nettie Lee. "Acquisition of Serials from Latin America." *Serial Slants* IV (July, 1953), pp. 110-114.

Bottaro, Raúl H. *La edición de libros en Argentina*. Buenos Aires: Ediciones Troquel [1964].

Bourjaily, Vance. "The Lost Books of Latin America." *Publishers Weekly* CLXXVII (April 11, 1960), pp. 14-15.

Boyd, Julian P. "A Landmark in the History of Library Cooperation in America." *College and Research Libraries* VIII (April, 1947), pp. 101-109.

Bradford, S. C. "Sources of Information on Specific Subjects." *Engineering* (January 26, 1934). British Society for International Bibliography. Publication Number 1. Reprint. 4 pp.

Cannon, Marie Willis. "Latin American Book Catalogues." In: *Handbook of Latin American Studies*, v. 7. Cambridge, Mass.: Harvard University Press, 1942, pp. 1-9.

Carnovsky, Leon, ed. *International Aspects of Librarianship*. [Chicago] The University of Chicago Press [1954]

Clapp, Verner W. "The Balance of Conflicting Interests in Building Collections—Comprehensiveness versus Selectivity." In: *Changing Patterns of Scholarship and the Future of Research Libraries: A Symposium in Celebration of the 200th Anniversary of the Establishment of the University of Pennsylvania Library*. Philadelphia: University of Pennsylvania Press, 1951, pp. 65-72.

Cline, Howard F. "Hispanica." *Library of Congress Quarterly Journal of Current Acquisitions* XI (November, 1953), pp. 46-59.

————. "Hispanica." *Library of Congress Quarterly Journal of Current Acquisitions* XIV (November, 1956), pp. 40-49.

————. "Latin America and the Farmington Plan: A Working Draft, with Recommendations." Hispanic Acquisitions Studies: 19. [Washington] Library of Congress, 1959. Xeroxed. 57 pp.

Collison, R. L. W. *Bibliographical Services throughout the World.* [Paris] UNESCO [1961]

————. *Bibliographies, Subject and National; A Guide to their Contents, Arrangement and Use.* 2nd ed. New York: Hafner Publishing Company, 1962.

Conover, Helen F. *Current National Bibliographies.* Washington: United States Government Printing Office, 1955.

————. "Records of Current Publishing in Latin America." In: *Handbook of Latin American Studies,* v. 22. Gainesville: University of Florida Press, 1960, pp. 327-329.

"Co-operative Provision of Books, Periodicals and Related Material in Libraries." Final Report of the Sub-Committee on Co-operative Provision of Books, Periodicals and Related Material in Libraries, and Statement of Policy, adopted by Council of the Library Association on 21st May, 1957. *Library Association Record* LIX (July, 1957), pp. 235-237.

Current Issues in Higher Education, 1965; Pressures and Priorities in Higher Education. Washington: Association for Higher Education [1965]

Daniels [Shepard] Marietta. "Bibliographic Activities of the Organization of American States." *American Library Association Bulletin* LX (July-August, 1961), pp. 635-640.

————. "The Contribution of the Organization of American States to the Exchange of Publications in the Americas." *Library Quarterly* XXVIII (January, 1958), pp. 45-55.

————. "The Inter-American Program for Library and Bibliographic Development of the Organization of American States." *Libri* XII (1962), pp. 139-145.

————. *The Seminars on the Acquisition of Latin American Library Materials: A Seven-Year Report, 1956-1962.* Washington: Pan American Union, 1962.

de la Garza, Peter. "Records of Current Publication in Bolivia, Ecuador, and Honduras." In: *Handbook of Latin American Studies,* v. 23. Gainesville: University of Florida Press, 1961, pp. 408-411.

Downs, Robert B. "Doctoral Programs and Library Resources." *College and Research Libraries* XXVII (March, 1966), pp. 123-129, 141.

————. "Library Cooperation and Specialization." In: *Problems and Prospects of the Research Library.* Association of Research Libraries. Edwin E. Williams, ed. New Brunswick, N. J.: The Scarecrow Press, 1955, pp. 91-104.

134   LACAP—An Imaginative Venture

————. "Report on Farmington Plan Program." Report to Council on Library Resources on Grant Received by the Association of Research Libraries for its Farmington Plan Program. *College and Research Libraries* XXIII (March, 1962), pp. 143-145.

————. "Wartime Co-operative Acquisitions." *Library Quarterly* XIX (July, 1949), pp. 157-165.

Drennan, Henry T. "Cooperative Selection and Book Ordering." In: *Selection and Acquisition Procedures in Medium-Sized and Large Libraries.* Herbert Goldhor, ed. Champaign, Illinois: The Illini Union Bookstore, 1963, pp. 55-70.

Esterquest, Ralp T. "Aspects of Library Cooperation." *College and Research Libraries* XIX (May, 1958), pp. 203-208.

————. ed. "Building Library Resources through Cooperation." Introduction. *Library Trends* VI (January, 1958), pp. 257-259.

Evans, Luther H. "National Library Resources." *Library Journal* LXXII (January 1, 1947), pp. 7-13, 71.

Fall, John. "Problems of American Libraries in Acquiring Foreign Publications." *Library Quarterly* XXIV (January, 1954), pp. 101-113.

Fussler, Herman H. "A New Pattern for Library Co-operation." *Library Journal* LXXXI (January 15, 1956), pp. 126-133.

García, Eustasio Antonio. *Desarrollo de la industria editorial argentina.* Buenos Aires: Fundación Interamericana de Bibliotecología Franklin [1965]

"The 'Get-'Em-All' Theory of Book Buying." *Library Journal* LXXXV (October 1, 1960), pp. 3387-3393.

Gonzalez, Manuel P. *Intellectual Relations between the United States and Spanish America,* lecture in California University, University of California. Committee on International Relations. *The Civilization of the Americas.* Berkeley: University of California, 1938, pp. 101-137. Quoted by Laurence J. Kipp in *The International Exchange of Publications.* [Wakefield, Mass.: Murray Printing Company, 1950] p. 44.

Harrison, John P. "Latin American Studies: Library Needs and Problems." In: *Area Studies and the Library; The Thirtieth Annual Conference of the Graduate Library School.* Tsuen Hsuin Tsien and Howard D. Winger, ed. Chicago: Chicago University Press, 1966, pp. 128-140.

Hilton, Ronald, ed. *Handbook of Hispanic Source Materials and Research Organizations in the United States.* 2nd ed. Stanford, Calif.: Stanford University Press, 1956.

Hutton, R. S. "Library Accessions: Some Questions of Selection and Coverage and the Farmington Plan." *Journal of Documentation* V (June, 1949), pp. [12]-18. Reprint.

"The Inter-American Program of Library and Bibliographic Development of the Organization of American States: A Statement of Principles and Practices." Cuadernos bibliotecológicos No. 11. Washington: Pan American Union, 1962. Mimeographed. 5 pp.

International Federation of Library Associations. *Libraries in the World.* The Hague: Martinus Nijhoff, 1963.

Jennison, Peter S., and Kurth, William H. *Books in the Americas: A Study of the Principal Barriers to the Booktrade in the Americas.* Washington: Pan American Union, 1960.

Kipp, Laurence J. *The International Exchange of Publications.* [Wakefield, Mass.: Murray Printing Company, 1950]

Klasse, Isay. "Facetas de la industria editorial mexicana." *Fichero Bibliográfico Hispanoamericano* V (November, 1965), pp. 42-45.

Kurth, William H. "Report of the Cooperative Library Mission to Latin America (September-December, 1958), Including Field Reports." Washington: Library of Congress, 1959. Photo-offset. About 350 pp.

Linder, Leroy Harold. *The Rise of Current Complete National Bibliography.* New York: The Scarecrow Press, 1959.

McNiff, Philip J. "Foreign Area Studies and Their Effect on Library Development." *College and Research Libraries* XXIV (July, 1963), pp. 291-296, 304-305.

————. "Harvard's Position on Blanket Orders and *En Bloc* Purchases." *Library Journal* LXXXVI (January 15, 1961), pp. 146-147.

Malclès, Louise-Noëlle. *Bibliographical Services throughout the World.* [Paris] UNESCO [1955]

————. *Manuel de bibliographie.* Paris: Presses Universitaires de France, 1963.

Melcher, Daniel. "Bookfinding in the Americas." *Library Journal* LXXXVI (November 15, 1961), pp. 3908-[3812]

Metcalf, Keyes D., and Williams, Edwin E. "Proposal for a Division of Responsibility among American Libraries in the Acquisition and Recording of Library Materials." *College and Research Libraries* V (March, 1944), pp. 105-109.

Moon, Eric. "The Sanctity of Book Selection." Editorial. *Library Journal* LXXXV (October 1, 1960), p. 3400.

Orne, Jerrold. "Storage and Deposit Libraries." *College and Research Libraries* XXI (November, 1960), pp. 446-452, 461.

Parry Report. *See* University Grants Committee. *Report of the Committee on Latin American Studies.*

Peñalosa, Fernando. *The Mexican Book Industry.* New York: The Scarcecrow Press, 1957.

————. *La selección y adquisición de libros; manual para bibliotecas.* Washington: Pan American Union, 1961.

Randall, William M., ed. *The Acquisition and Cataloging of Books.* Papers presented before the Library Institute at the University of Chicago, July 29 to August 9, 1940. Chicago: University of Chicago Press [ᶜ1940]

Rider, Fremont. *The Scholar and the Future of the Research Library.* New York City: Hadham Press, 1944.

Sabor, Josefa E. "La bibliografía general argentina en curso de publicación." In: *Handbook of Latin American Studies,* v. 25. Gainesville: University of Florida Press, 1963, pp. 374-379.

"Statistical Analysis of Sixty-two ARL Academic Libraries 1951-52—1961-62." Association of Research Libraries. *Minutes of the Sixty-third Meeting of the Association of Research Libraries, January 23, 1964, Chicago, Illinois.* Appendix D, p. 47.

Stevens, Rolland E. "Library Support for Area Study Programs." *College and Research Libraries* XXIV (September, 1963), pp. 383-391.

Talmadge, Robert H. "The Farmington Plan." *Canadian Library Association Bulletin* XVI (March, 1960), pp. 209-212.

————. "The Farmington Plan Survey; An Interim Report." *College and Research Libraries* XIX (September, 1958), pp. 375-383.

Tauber, Maurice F., and Associates. *Technical Services in Libraries.* New York: Columbia University Press, 1953.

Trade Barriers to Knowledge: A Manual of Regulations Affecting Educational Scientific and Cultural Materials. 2nd ed. Paris: UNESCO [1955]

Turner, Mary. "Una ayuda para bibliotecas." *Fichero Bibliográfico Hispanoamericano* V (April, 1966), p. 28.

United Nations Educational, Scientific and Cultural Organization. *Handbook on the International Exchange of Publications.* 3rd. ed. Gisela von Busse, ed. [Paris] UNESCO [1964]

University Grants Committee. *Report of the Committee on Latin American Studies.* London: Her Majesty's Stationery Office, 1965. [Parry Report]

U. S. Department of State. *Resources Survey of Latin American Countries.* [Washington] 1965.

Vosper, Robert. "Farmington Redivivus: Or Ten Years of Coordinated Foreign Book Procurement in the U. S." Address delivered at the 34th Annual Conference of the Library Association, Scarborough, 5th October, 1959. *Aslib Proceedings* XI (December, 1959), pp. 327-332.

————. *The Farmington Plan Survey: A Summary of the Separate Studies of 1957-1961.* University of Illinois Graduate School of Library Science. Occasional Papers. No. 77. October 1965. Urbana. Illinois; University of Illinois Graduate School of Library Science [1965]

————. "International Book Procurement; Or Farmington Extended." *College and Research Libraries* XXI (March, 1960), pp. 117-124.

Walford, A. J. "Bibliographical Organization and Bibliographies." In: *Five Years' Work in Librarianship, 1956-1960.* London: Library Association, 1963, pp. 329-356.

Wasley, John S. W. "The Book Trade in Latin America: A Survey of Basic Problems." *Publishers Weekly* CLXXIII (March 3, 1958) pp. 16-19, and (March 10, 1958), pp. 26-[30]

West, Stanley L., "Acquisition of Library Materials from Latin America." *Library Resources and Technical Services* VII (Winter, 1963), pp. 7-12.

Williams, Edwin E. *Farmington Plan Handbook.* [Cambridge, Mass.] Association of Research Libraries, 1953.

————. *Farmington Plan Handbook, Revised to 1961 and Abridged.* [Cambridge, Mass.] Association of Research Libraries, 1961.

————. "Research Library Acquisitions from Eight Countries." *Library Quarterly* XV (October, 1945), pp. 313-323.

————. "Some Questions on Three Cooperative Projects." *Library Trends* I (July, 1952), pp. 156-165.

Wise, Murray M. "Development of Bibliographical Activity during the Past Five Years: A Tentative Survey." In: *Handbook of Latin American Studies,* v. 5. Cambridge, Mass.: Harvard University Press, 1940, pp. 13-26.

Index